JUDAS

JUDAS

Clifton J. Brown

To order additional copies of this book, contact:
Xlibris Corporation
1-888-795-4274
www.Xlibris.com
Orders@Xlibris.com
17970

CONTENTS

IDENTIFICATION 7
ACKNOWLEDGEMENT 9
PREFACE 11
APOLOGY 13
CHAPTER 1
    BOYHOOD EVENT 15
CHAPTER 2
    PUBLICAN 19
CHAPTER 3
    DISCIPLE 26
CHAPTER 4
    CHOSEN APOSTLE 28
CHAPTER 5
    MIRACLES 31
CHAPTER 6
    TAMAR...34
CHAPTER 7
    SIMON, THE PHARISEE.....................................54
CHAPTER 8
    STORM 56
CHAPTER 9
    JAIRUS 63
CHAPTER 10
    NAZARETH 68
CHAPTER 11
    FIRST KINGDOM CAMPAIGN 72
CHAPTER 12
    MAKING A KING 83
CHAPTER 13

THE BEGINNING CANCER 90
CHAPTER 14
CANNIBALISM 95
CHAPTER 15
GENTILE COUNTRY 99
CHAPTER 16
SIN, UNCONFESSED 103
CHAPTER 17
EPHER 110
CHAPTER 18
THE COLD MOUNTAIN 113
CHAPTER 19
DISSENSION 117
CHAPTER 20
ELIHU 120
CHAPTER 21
THE GREAT GULF 127
CHAPTER 22
DEATH OF A FRIEND 131
CHAPTER 23
YOUR BROTHER SHALL RISE AGAIN 133
CHAPTER 24
CEDRON 139
CHAPTER 25
ON THE JERICHO ROAD 143
CHAPTER 26
ZACCHAEUS 145
CHAPTER 27
THE BEGINNING OF THE END 148
CHAPTER 28
THE KING IS COMING 154
CHAPTER 29
COUNTDOWN TO MISERY 157
CHAPTER 30
POINT OF NO RETURN 171
CHAPTER 31
HORRIBLE DEATH 175

IDENTIFICATION

My name is Clifton Brown. I never intended to be a writer. I graduated from Tennessee Temple College with a Bachelor of Arts degree with a major in Bible. After forty years in the ministry, I retired and was impressed to write a book about Judas. My first draft was with pencil and paper. I later took a correspondence course from The Long Ridge writer's school in Connecticut.

AKNOWLEDGEMENT

My research has been limited to my own library and the Bible. I have sometimes copied prayers and excerpts from *The Life and Times of Jesus the Messiah*. Erdmans Publishers.

I want to thank my youngest daughter, Cathy, and my oldest daughter, Connie, for encouraging me to finish this book.

PREFACE

Common conception portrays Judas Iscariot as a sinister, shadowy character that no one would trust. Such a person would cause people to feel uneasy in his presence. It is not logical that the little group of twelve apostles that Jesus chose to train for the all-important task of carrying the good news to all the world would have accepted such a person to carry their money, nor is it likely that Jesus would have chosen someone in whom the rest would have no confidence.

Jesus treated Judas as a trusted friend and none of the other disciples suspected that he would betray Jesus, although Jesus plainly foretold the event. I believe that most of the time, he went quietly about his work of distributing to the poor. He may have received some admiration from the poor as an agent of the Group's benevolence.

The source and the amount of money handled by Judas can, of course, be only a matter of conjecture. Jesus would not have accepted any fees for his ministry even if the recipients could have paid. Some, out of gratitude, may have pressed small sums upon the Group. While there may have been wealthy people among the larger group of disciples, it is doubtful that any of the Twelve had more than moderate means.

Jesus told the rich, young ruler to sell all that he had and give to the poor. For the ruler, this was prerequisite to discipleship because his wealth was an obsession. Not all wealthy people were asked to do this because Jesus deals with people on an individual basis. There may have been other greedy persons who, unlike the rich, young ruler, gladly gave up their possessions to follow Jesus. No matter, from whatever source, Judas handled a sizeable sum of money.

There must have been a required audit of the account periodically. To believe otherwise would be to assume that the disciples were slipshod and careless with the money entrusted to them, not at all in keeping with Christ's teaching. I believe that in the beginning Judas was conscientious in his task.

Embezzlement is not a violent crime. Some very respectable people have found that they could divert small sums of public money to their own use and later replace it without anyone knowing it. It can easily become a loan in the thinking of the offender. No embezzler deliberately intends to be a thief.

Judas was not some fictitious character out of some horror movie, but an actual living person with all the desires, ambitions, and drives common to mankind. He was not a helpless pawn, but a rational man capable of making his own decisions. His decision to betray Christ was not a sudden one, but the culmination of many prior flawed decisions springing from the foul fountain of unbelief. All unredeemed human beings are capable of actions similar to Judas'. Only the grace of God, which was offered to him repeatedly, stands between us and Judas' fate.

It is my hope that the reader may ask himself the same question that all asked at the Last Supper: "Is it I, Lord?"

APOLOGY

This book is fiction. Some of the events described actually happened, but absolute accuracy has not been attempted. However, the life of Judas was so interwoven with the Gospel of Jesus Christ that the reader may profit by comparing with the Bible.

Some of the discrepancies are unintentional. However, I am aware that my version of Judas' suicide is contradictory to Matthew 27:5. My own perception is based on Acts 1:18 and is pure imagination added to increase drama.

.

CHAPTER 1

BOYHOOD EVENT

When Judas was eight years old his mother, Eshton, said to his father, Bidkar, "I'm going to make a ketonet for Judas. He is getting too old for a tunic, especially since he only plays with Deborah." Deborah was Judas' cousin, who lived in the same village of Kerioth. In fact, he could see her house by climbing a sycamore fig tree that grew nearby.

"I'll buy him a yarmulke at the market, and he can go with us to the temple," said Bidkar.

Eshton made the ketonet out of blue, red, yellow, green and black cloth. She sewed it together in strips, and when it was finished it looked like the coat that Jacob had given to Joseph. Judas felt grown up in his new attire, but it hampered him in climbing his favorite tree to see Deborah's house. Bidkar showed him how to pull the skirts of the garment up between his legs and tie them at his waist with a girdle.

Judas also had a problem with his yarmulke. Curls framed his face when he wore it, giving him a girlish appearance. It was embarrassing to him, but Deborah was envious. She kept her long and straight hair plaited around her head, but it would have been nice to have curls like Judas.

At fourteen, she was a head taller than Judas. A prominent nose and high cheekbones gave her a plain appearance, but her bubbly disposition animated her face and charmed her friends. The long garment she wore, though similar to Judas' ketonet except for the added needlework, hid her fully mature form.

She and Judas were inseparable. They spent hours talking and playing together, which was unusual because boys his age generally detested girls, and girls shared secrets only with other girls. She seemed more like an older sister than a cousin. Judas' brother Jotham was a pest, and his sister Adah hadn't been born yet.

Deborah had been betrothed at the age of ten. Judas was too young to know what it meant, but Deborah had explained that a man had made arrangements with her father for her to marry his son, Laban, when they reached the marriageable age. She had seen Laban one time and had been delighted with what she saw. He was handsome and tall, just like all girls dream about. When he learned his father's pottery trade, they would be married.

"Oh, Judas, I can hardly wait. He is so handsome and strong," Deborah bubbled with happiness. Judas had not understood being in love, but if Laban could make his cousin and friend this happy, then he was sure that he would like Laban, although the idea of Deborah moving away made him sad.

One day, when Deborah came visiting, Judas sensed something was troubling her. She soon told him. "Father borrowed money from a rich man and he can't pay it back. He may have to sell me as a servant."

"Why doesn't he sell Eglah?" Judas was speaking of Deborah's younger sister.

"She is too young to work."

"There should be some other way."

"The rich man is coming tomorrow."

The following day, a man wearing me-il, turban, and soft leather shoes rode a black horse to Deborah's house. Judas climbed his sycamore fig tree so he could see and not be seen. The man entered the house, and after some time Deborah's mother and father and Eglah and Adinah came out and went down the street toward their field, but the black horse remained tied to a post beside their house. Later the man came out and rode away. Judas sensed that something was wrong, but he had no idea what.

Deborah didn't come over to talk anymore. Judas went to her house once, but her mother told him that Deborah was too old to play with him. Occasionally he would see her carrying water pots or grinding corn, but that was the only time he even caught a glimpse of her. The man on the black horse came often. Deborah's parents and sisters were always at work in the fields. Judas wondered if maybe Deborah's father had paid off the debt to the rich man, because her sisters went with her parents and Deborah worked around the house. Maybe Adinah and Eglah would come over and tell him. They were nearer his age than Deborah, but he had never liked them. Adinah was a little chatterbox and Eglah looked like an overgrown squab.

Just before his ninth birthday, they did come over to his home, overjoyed with news. "Judas, there is going to be a wedding at our house!" Eglah exclaimed.

Before she could say more, Adinah burst out, "Deborah is going to get married and we're going to be virgins and carry lamps and meet the bridegroom and everything!" Nor was the excitement limited to Adinah and Eglah. The entire village was in eager anticipation. Wedding festivities could last one or two weeks and everyone in the village was invited.

Judas, of course, went to the wedding, but it seemed more like a funeral than a wedding. Laban, the bridegroom, escorted by his friends, was met by the virgins (Adinah and Eglah among them), and seemed in a joyful mood as befitting the occasion. However, Deborah's parents wore the countenance of ones in mourning when Laban received his bride from them. Deborah herself acted like one condemned. Of course, nine-year-old Judas did not understand the implications of the adults' behavior. Laban's friends from Jerusalem drank enormous quantities of wine and ate endless portions of cakes and figs and muttons and fatted calf. But Deborah's parents, Jacob and Leah, ate little and Deborah ate nothing at all. It was the first time that Judas had seen Deborah's face since the day of the rich man's visit. She was haggard and thin, only a shadow of her former self.

The wedding was over and Laban had taken his bride and returned to Jerusalem. A day or two later they came back, and a group of twelve priests accompanied the party. After a lot of excited talking to Deborah's parents, the elders of Iscariot went to each house in the village. When they came to Judas' house, he overheard his father say, "I'll not have any part in it. According to our laws, they are both to be stoned, and according to Roman law, we Jews are not allowed to administer the death penalty."

"She refuses to tell who it is. The priests have already found her guilty, and as long as there is not a riot, the Romans won't care about a stoning," was the reply given by the village elder who had come to their house.

Judas would never forget the look of terror on Deborah's face as she was led from the house between the two priests. He slipped out the back way and followed the crowd to the edge of the village. Because of the crowd he couldn't see what was happening, but he could hear.

It was the same sound that he had heard at the temple when the priest knocked down the animal for the evening sacrifice. There was a thud, followed by a piercing scream, then a succession of thumps more muffled than the first. Finally, there was the ringing sound of stone upon stone. The crowd dispersed quietly, subdued and ashamed of what they had thought necessary: executing the law without mercy. Laban was crying openly. Only the priests seemed unmoved by the experience.

After the crowd had dispersed, only a mound of stones that had become Deborah's sepulchre remained.

CHAPTER 2

PUBLICAN

(Fifteen years later)

Judas was getting anxious. It was midday and no one had stopped at his booth to pay taxes. Aijalon was a day late. He usually stopped fourteen days after he had passed by the booth on the way from Jericho to Egypt.

Although it was not Judas' policy to charge both ways as some of his fellow publicans did, he did want to collect from Aijalon on his way back to Damascus. Aijalon was a wealthy trader, who owned four dromedary camels, the only camel-owning trader paying taxes at Judas' booth.

Local traders used burros instead of camels. Although a camel could carry a heavier load than a burro, the mountainous terrain of Palestine made camels impractical. Aijalon unloaded his camels at Capernaum and took a string of ten burros to Damascus.

Judas had been looking forward to collecting from Aijalon. He always went up to Jerusalem for a little dice game the night after he collected from him. He never won a lot of money, but he enjoyed playing.

"Shalom, Judas," Akhub greeted Judas as he stopped with his string of burros to pay his taxes.

"Shalom, Akhub," Judas greeted the trader. "You are early. Aijalon usually passes here before you do."

"Aijalon is ahead of me. He left Hebron almost a day ahead of me."

"I didn't see him, and I was here all day yesterday."

"He must have passed through last night. That lead camel of his can see in the dark."

"I never heard of a camel that could see at night."

"Dromedaries can; they can cover one hundred fifty miles in a twenty-four hour day." Akhub paid the customary fee and went on his way.

Soon after Akhub had gone, Casper, the Roman tax supervisor, rode up on a white horse. Judas had collected enough to give him the Roman percentage, but he was seething over Aijalon's deception.

"That crafty devil Aijalon slipped through last night without paying his taxes," complained Judas.

"We can't let him get away with *that*," Casper chuckled. "We will catch him at Capernaum, but you will have to go with me to testify against him."

"But I can't leave my toll booth," Judas protested. He knew five or six other Jews who would like his job. The Roman government contracted tax-collecting to indigenous entrepreneurs to avoid direct confrontation with the populace. A "publican" was classified with sinners by loyal Jews, but the job was lucrative. He could charge over and above the Roman requirement and the soldiers would enforce it. It was a political job obtained by bribery. Judas had obtained it by paying all of his inheritance from his father's estate.

"I'll get Hilen to occupy your booth until you return. Don't worry, he will surrender it when you return," Casper said, anticipating Judas' objection. Casper returned the next morning with Hilen.

"You can ride double with me," Casper said. "My horse is strong. We will arrive in Capernaum by nightfall."

They did, indeed, arrive in Capernaum by nightfall. Casper found a livery stable for his horse and lodging at a nearby inn. Judas exhausted his finances to secure his lodging and could not join in the dice game going on in the back room. Casper offered him a loan against the sum he would collect from Aijalon, but Judas had learned long ago not to gamble with borrowed money.

The next day, they went to look for Aijalon. They found him in the marketplace trying to sell an Egyptian pot.

"See the fine gold etchings around the rim, and look at the picture engraved on the side. Not at all like our plain Jewish pots," Aijalon urged.

"But isn't that an image of Ra, the sun god?" the customer asked.

Judas interrupted the transaction by confronting Aijalon. "You did not pay your taxes. You slipped by my booth at night while I was sleeping."

"I did pay my taxes. You are just trying to collect twice. Everybody knows that camels can't travel at night."

Casper gave a hand signal. Two Roman soldiers on horses appeared. "If Judas says you didn't pay taxes, you didn't pay taxes," Casper said firmly.

"Oh, my poor mother, and she a widow and I the only son to care for her. My children, they will have nothing to eat tonight," Aijalon complained loudly, as he counted out the usual tribute.

"You are forgetting something. Judas was forced to leave his booth in the care of Hilen and come to Capernaum to collect. Double the money," Casper said.

Aijalon was stunned into silence, but looking again at the mounted soldiers, he counted out five more coins.

"That is much better," Casper said. "You just delivered yourself from prison."

As they left the marketplace, Casper told Judas, "We won't go back down to Jericho until tomorrow."

"Take the extra money that I collected from Aijalon for bringing me up here, and half of what he owed me for your soldier friends," Judas said. He knew that the Romans loved bribes, and he wanted to stay in good favor with them. Casper accepted his offer and left with his friends.

With nothing to do and very little money, Judas wandered back to the marketplace.

"Shalom, Judas!" shouted Matthew, a fellow publican, whom Judas had met a year before when Matthew had stopped at Jericho on his way to Jerusalem to observe the Passover. Matthew managed a tax booth in Capernaum, and by sharing their common experiences, they had become good friends.

"Shalom, Matthew," Judas returned the greeting with genuine pleasure.

"How is your mother, Eshton?" Matthew asked.

"She is well," Judas replied.

"And your brother, Jotham?"

"He is well."

"Your younger sister?"

"Alas, she is no more. After the feast of tabernacles, she died of a fever." Judas' chin began to quiver and tears came to his eyes. He had been very fond of his little sister, and had grieved more for her than for his father, who had been a good man and a wise father.

Common courtesy would have required Judas to ask about the health of Matthew's family, but Matthew had news that couldn't wait.

"Judas, I want you to meet the most extraordinary person I've ever known, Jesus of Nazareth. He is coming to my house for supper tonight, and I have invited all the publicans in Capernaum. Could you come?" Matthew asked hopefully.

"Casper is taking me back to Jericho tomorrow, but I can come to your feast tonight. I have heard of this Jesus of Nazareth, and I would like to see him."

"Then you will come. Why don't you come with me now? I have already purchased a fatted calf, and my servant is even now roasting it for tonight," Matthew urged. "Since you won't go to Jericho until tomorrow, you can spend the night at my house." Judas was glad to accept Matthew's hospitality.

Before sunset, people began coming into Matthew's courtyard. They made no attempt to come into the dining area. It was obvious that they weren't invited guests, but had come out of curiosity. Judas was surprised to see some scribes and Pharisees among those who had come, since it would be a sin for them to eat with a publican. However, the dining area was open to the courtyard, and they could see and hear the diners without participating in the feast.

At the appointed time, Jesus and his disciples arrived and reclined around the table. Jesus was given a place facing the courtyard and Judas had a place next to Matthew facing Jesus.

"Why are you, who go about teaching in Israel, eating with publicans and sinners?" Judas heard a voice behind him speaking. Obviously, the question was addressed to Jesus, but Judas knew that it was about him and Matthew. He felt shame and anger at the same time. His own family had strongly disapproved of his becoming a tax collector, although poverty had forced them to accept money from him. They really wouldn't care if he never came back to Kerioth, well, at least not to Jericho.

"They that are well don't need a doctor. Only those who are sick," Jesus answered the Pharisee. "I didn't come to call the righteous, but sinners to repentance."

Judas wasn't sure what Jesus meant by that statement, but it made him feel better. He liked the way Jesus thwarted the pompous Pharisee's thrust. He himself had been the object of the Pharisees' scorn since he began collecting taxes for the Roman government. He enjoyed his work. It gave him an opportunity to handle money, a natural talent for him.

After Jesus and the other disciples had gone, Matthew asked a question of Judas, "Would you be interested in becoming a disciple of Jesus?"

"I have to go back to Jericho tomorrow. Hilen will be expecting me," Judas said.

"Hilen is probably hoping you won't come back at all. He has been wanting that booth for three years. Why don't you stay in Capernaum?"

"You mean I should give up my business to follow Jesus?"

"That is what I have done."

"How are you going to make a living?"

"The same as the rest of the disciples. Peter, James and John left their fishing business to follow Jesus."

"I don't know. I have my family to support."

"Jotham is old enough to work and take care of your mother. Have you seen them since Adah died?"

"No." Matthew's last question had started Judas thinking.

He knew they really didn't need him any more. Although he had given them enough to satisfy the law, it was only a token of his actual income. He lived in a modest home in Jericho, but it was a hovel in comparison to the homes of most publicans. He had squandered much of his money gambling.

"I believe that Jesus will be the king of the Jews someday," Matthew said.

"Why do you believe that?"

"I traced his lineage and it goes back to King David."

"But I thought Jesus was a Nazarene."

"He was born in Bethlehem, the city of David. His parents were of the house and lineage of David and were in Bethlehem registering to be taxed when Jesus was born. That was when Cyrenious was governor of Syria."

Matthew's mention of a kingdom interested Judas. "Then the followers of Jesus will have part in the kingdom when Jesus becomes king?"

"I hadn't thought of it, but yes, they would. Whether he becomes king or not, his teaching is as one who has authority and not as the scribes and Pharisees."

"What you say about Jesus is very interesting, but I have a good business in Jericho and your friend Jesus will not become king unless Caesar appoints him king, no matter if King David were still living."

Matthew stopped urging discipleship on Judas. "I will show you where you may sleep tonight," he said.

Judas marveled at the size of Matthew's house, which was in conformity with his position as chief publican. As he lay on the mat in the room that Matthew had shown him, he ran his options through his mind. The wisest thing for him to do would be to go back to Jericho to his lucrative tax collecting business. Still, it would be exciting to be involved in a new political movement. It would be dangerous. King Herod wouldn't take kindly to a new king. Herod wasn't as wicked as his father, Herod the Great, who had all the babies in Bethlehem killed because the magi and told him that the king of the Jews had been born in Bethlehem. Matthew had said that Jesus was born in Bethlehem, but it must have been after Herod the Great died. It was too great a risk. After Judas made his decision to go back to Jericho in the morning, he slept.

Early the next morning Judas awakened and hurried to the livery stable to wait for Casper, fearing that Casper would be impatient to get started to Jericho. The sun's rim was barely visible on the horizon when the slave, who tended the horses, came from his quarters.

Recognizing Judas as a common Jew who rode only donkeys, he pointed to another stable north of the first and said, "We keep the donkeys in yonder stable."

"Where is the white horse that belongs to Casper?" Judas asked.

"The master came for him yesterday," the slave answered.

Judas was stunned as the plot hit him. Hilen had bribed Casper to bring Judas to Capernaum. Casper didn't care whether he got his money from Aijalon. No point in going back to Jericho. Hilen occupied his booth, and Casper would not force him to return it to Judas. The only option remaining was to become a disciple of Jesus of Nazareth.

CHAPTER 3

DISCIPLE

"Where have you been? You are almost too late for breakfast," Matthew greeted Judas cheerily. "Help yourself to the cakes," Matthew added without waiting for an answer.

Judas had not realized how hungry he was. He ate with relish while his host watched with pride. When Judas had finished eating, Matthew asked, "Have you considered becoming a disciple of Jesus?"

"Yes, I will be a disciple," Judas answered. He didn't tell Matthew that Casper and Hilen had taken his booth away from him.

"Oh, that is wonderful!" Matthew cried. "Let's go tell Jesus now. He is staying with Hachilah, who is the mother of the wife of Simon, son of Jonas. She came to live with them after her husband died. Peter and Rachel had one son, Jonathon. They were overjoyed when Rachel became pregnant again, hoping to have a large family. Sadly it was not to be; Rachel died in childbirth and the baby was stillborn. Hachilah stayed on and kept house for Peter and Jonathon. She was too old to bear any more children, and would never marry again. And so it is that Peter supports his wife's mother, and Hachilah cares for Peter's orphaned son."

When they reached Hachilah's house, Jesus and his disciples had already gone north toward the mountains. When Matthew and Judas overtook Jesus and the other disciples, they were surrounded by a crowd of almost all common people: fishermen, farmers, shepherds, women and children. They were the poor and unlearned from the slums of Capernaum and the poor regions of the countryside. Judas almost felt guilty for the fine garments that he was wearing. However, everyone was friendly and welcoming. He no longer had to take the abuse by those from whom he collected taxes. The Romans for whom he worked despised him, and the Jewish officials hated him, making it clear that they expected him to burn in hell.

CHAPTER 4

CHOSEN APOSTLE

It was cool, but not cold, just invigorating when they awakened the next morning in the foothills of the Gallilean mountains. Jesus had been gone all night, but no one seemed alarmed. John said that Jesus always went away to pray after a day of healing and teaching, but he couldn't remember his being gone all night before. They had been waiting for him since dawn. While they were waiting, John had briefly filled them in on what Jesus had taught and done since he and Andrew had gone home with Jesus the day that John the Baptist had said, "Behold the Lamb of God that takes away the sins of the world." As Judas became better acquainted with Jesus' disciples, they described meeting Jesus as an experience rather than an introduction. It seemed that meeting Jesus was a life-changing experience. So engrossed was Judas in John's account of his experience with Jesus that he was startled when Jesus suddenly appeared in their midst after having been gone all night.

Jesus immediately began calling out the names of those selected to be apostles. Simon, who was later called Peter; Andrew, the one who introduced his brother, Simon, to Jesus; James and John (the sons of Thunder, old Zebedee's sons); Philip, who enlisted Nathaniel; Bartholomew, Nathaniel's other name; Thomas, the twin; Matthew (Judas was glad to hear his friend's name called); James, the son of Alphaeus; Lebbaeus, Thaddaeus; Simon, the Cannanite; and Judas of Iscariot! He could hardly believe his ears! Jesus was calling him to be one of the twelve apostles. He was in! Not only a disciple, but one of the elite twelve. He didn't know what all it involved, but it felt good to be included after all the abuse and scorn the Pharisees and Sadducees had given him.

Judas' reverie was broken by seeing Jesus climbing to a level place on the mountain. Jesus sat down on a boulder and the crowd sat or crouched, and the clamor became a mere murmur.

With the mountain as a backdrop, Jesus began to explain the principles of the Kingdom of Heaven: Happy are those who mourn. Judas hadn't been happy since his fatter had died five years ago, and Adah, who had been only twelve, just a year ago. Tears started in his eyes. What a beautiful child she had been. However, the necessity of living and time itself had taken the edge off grief and he really did feel happier than he had for a long time.

There was something about Jesus, maybe his smile, that made you feel that you were somebody important. Judas didn't understand all that Jesus was saying, but it was nice to be called "friend," the word Jesus used the first time he saw him. He hadn't had many friends in his lifetime.

Now Jesus was saying the meek are happy. Jesus must be naïve. Meekness would not have saved his tax booth. Going to inherit the earth? Jesus must be dreaming. The Romans ruled all the world that he knew anything about, and they were anything but meek. Yet Matthew had said that Jesus was in line to inherit the kingdom of David. It wouldn't hurt to get in on it.

Now, what did he mean? Hunger and thirst after righteousness? He knew what it was to be hungry and thirsty, but he couldn't figure wanting to be righteous that much.

Happy are the merciful. Evidently, Jesus had never lived in the real world. One could try to be fair, but one couldn't be merciful. Debts had to be paid and somebody had to pay them. Mercy had to be limited to those who could and would pay with a little more time. Mercy sounded good, but it just didn't work.

Happy are the pure in heart. Judas agreed that it would be wonderful to have a pure heart. He had seen so much sin and ugliness that he just wished sometimes that he could take some water and wash his insides.

Love your enemies. Impossible! Judas didn't want to love his enemies. He didn't dare love his enemies. He had made a lot of enemies collecting taxes for the Roman government. They were out to get him. Even if he weren't a disciple, he would be afraid to go back to Jericho. No longer a publican, the Roman soldiers would have no interest in protecting him from his enemies.

He wished that Jesus would finish with the teaching and start performing miracles. He didn't understand what Jesus was talking about and was not really all that interested. Praying, fasting, almsgiving, that was the priests' job. That was what they got paid for, and they really seemed to enjoy doing it. He had seen them standing on street corners, praying, dour expressions on their faces from their continual fasting. Beggars could expect a few coins from them on feast days when there was a crowd around.

Now Jesus was saying that in the new Kingdom of Heaven no one would have to worry about food, clothing and shelter. God would take care of them. He didn't know what birds and lilies had to do with it. Maybe like the ravens fed Elijah in the great drought.

CHAPTER 5

MIRACLES

As they descended the mountain, the crowd suddenly stopped and began shrinking back. Only Jesus continued on to meet the leper hobbling toward them. Judas could hardly bear to look at the man. His entire body was covered with festering, seeping sores. The disease had erased the features of his face. His hands were mere stubs with nubs for fingers. A few old rags covered his nakedness. He emitted a piteous cry, "Lord, if you will, you can make me clean."

No sane man would have dared do what Jesus did! He touched the leper and said, "I will, be clean."

Judas was incredulous. The sores were all gone. The leper had a nose, fingers and toes. He still wore the same old rags, but otherwise that man was completely different in appearance than he had been a moment before. It couldn't be, but it was. This was what Judas had heard about. This was it! A Miracle! Jesus had worked a miracle.

As they were approaching the city, they met a Roman soldier. Judas was annoyed. A Roman soldier never approached a Jew unless he wanted him to carry his gear. He could make him carry it a mile. Jesus had said, "Carry it two miles." They might be carrying all night because this soldier was a centurion and he might want the gear of one hundred soldiers carried. However, the soldier only wanted Jesus to heal his sick slave. He must have been a valuable slave because Romans usually didn't care whether a slave lived or died.

"I will come and heal him," Jesus said. What kind of talk is that, Judas wondered? It was good that Jesus could heal, but this was carrying it too far. He himself had collected taxes for the Romans, but he didn't associate with them any more than he had to. No telling where that centurion lived. He might be stationed at Capernaum, but he also might live a day's journey away. Judas was tired. He might just let the rest of them go with the centurion.

"That won't be necessary," Judas heard the centurion say. "I am not worthy for you to come under my roof. Just speak the word and my slave will be healed. Like you, I am a man under authority. The soldiers under my command do whatever I say."

Jesus turned to them and said, "I haven't found this much faith in Israel. Many will come from the East and from the West and shall sit down with Abraham and Isaac and Jacob in the Kingdom of Heaven. But the children of the Kingdom shall be cast into outer darkness; there shall be weeping and gnashing of teeth."

Jesus turned back to the centurion. "Go your way. As you have believed, so shall it be."

Judas felt better. At least they wouldn't have to go to that man's house tonight. They went to Peter's home to eat and sleep.

Peter went inside to announce their arrival, but soon came back out.

"My mother-in-law is sick. She was all right when I left this morning," he explained. She lay moaning on a mat just off the dining hall. Her cheeks were flushed with fever. Jesus went in and touched her hand. She sat up with a surprised look on her face.

"Oh, I didn't expect you so soon," she said apologetically.

Hurriedly she arose and served them. Although Peter and her husband were fishermen, Hachilah had purchased a lamb and had dressed and cooked it for the guests while she was sick with the fever. When she had made everything ready, she left the room. The day had been long and Judas couldn't remember having eaten that morning, which greatly added to the enjoyment of the meal. When they had finished eating, Jesus offered a prayer of thanksgiving and was gone. The rest went out into the courtyard and gathered around the cooking fire, for the night was a bit chilly from the moderate breeze from the western mountains.

"Where is Jesus?" asked Judas.

"He has gone back up into the mountains to pray," John said. "He prays every night, sometimes until dawn. Even when he doesn't pray all night, he may get up before dawn and go back again."

"I should think he would be so tired and sleepy that he couldn't do anything in the daytime," Judas observed.

"That is where he gets his power to do miracles," Peter broke into the conversation.

"I had heard that he could do all kinds of amazing things," said Judas. "But I had never seen him do any until today."

Peter needed no further encouragement. He began with his brother Andrew's call, and continued to tell about the things that Jesus had said and done to the present, but Judas didn't hear him. He was asleep.

Early the next morning Jesus aroused the twelve apostles. Noticing that only the twelve chosen were with them, Judas remarked, "Not as many people as yesterday."

"That is why we started early," Philip replied. "Jesus wants to go to all the villages and towns we can before the kingdom comes."

CHAPTER 6

TAMAR

When Tamar was twelve years old she was fully mature. From under her kaffiyeh, raven black hair flowed to her waist. Almond eyes said, "Hey, I'm here. I like you and we can be friends." A smile constantly tugged at the corners of her mouth. A soft olive complexion completed a picture of young feminine beauty verging on womanhood. Adding to her charm was her unawareness of her attractiveness.

Her father, Diklah, had no sons, a near tragedy for a Jewish farmer. Therefore, he was delighted when, at the age of five, Tamar followed him to the fields on sturdy little legs. As her childhood years passed, they became a father-daughter team, and he was loathe to give his virgin daughter in marriage, although a wealthy neighbor had approached him with a marriage offer for her and his son.

She and her mother, Adah, however, did not have as close a relationship. Dutifully, but without enthusiasm, Tamar ran errands for her mother when she wasn't helping Diklah. One such errand exposed her to the undesirable elements of Capernaum. Although a mere two miles from her home, Capernaum was a different world. A commercial city located at the head of Lake Galilee and on a trade route from Egypt to Syria, it attracted a variety of profitable enterprises, both good and bad.

The market, or agora, was the civic center where people gathered for recreation, where the unemployed loafed, and where the proud paraded. Fishermen, farmers, and craftsmen from surrounding communities; traders and merchants from afar; and the ever-present Roman soldiers thronged the marketplace. Tamar jostled her way

through the throng until she found the stall selling spices. Adah
had given her ten assarin to buy mint and cumin, but when she
asked the price of the cumin, she was unprepared for the answer.

"I picked it fresh this morning. I have to have thirty assarin for
it," the seedy little man said. In Tamar's mind the only option was
to go back home for more money. Her mother must not have known
how much she would have to pay.

As she turned away he called, "Wait! To a beautiful young lady
like you I might sell it for twenty." Tamar began to understand
that the gap between asking price and purchase price could be
narrowed. She picked up a handful of cumin and examined it closely.
"It doesn't look like very good cumin to me, but I might give you
five assarin for it."

"Five? Are you beside yourself? You're not supposed to look at
cumin, you taste it!" the man stormed. "Fifteen is absolutely the
least that I can sell it for."

Sensing that the ten assarin her mother had given her was the
fair price, Tamar said, "If you'll put a handful of mint with it, I'll
give you ten, but not an assarin more."

"So soon the beautiful young lady becomes an ugly old hag,"
he replied, dropping flattery for demeaning words, and gave her
the spices in exchange for the money.

As Tamar turned away from the stall, she bumped into a
pleasant-looking, middle-aged man. "I'm sorry," she said as she
averted her eyes and stepped around him.

"I'm not. It is a pleasure to accidentally bump into a pretty
girl. This is my lucky day."

His words caught her off-guard. A man didn't speak to a woman
in public. His next words were even more puzzling. "Would you
like to go for a boat ride?"

"Were you speaking to me?"

"Of course. You've never ridden in a boat, have you?"

"No, but I don't know you. How do I know that you will
bring me back?"

"You don't. You'll just have to take my word for it. It's up to
you. Do you want to sail with me?"

She knew she shouldn't, but a kind of recklessness overrode caution. She had always been a good girl, she deserved some fun, she thought. "I'll go."

It was fun. After rowing some distance from shore, the man raised the sail. A steady, moderate breeze caught the sail and they started moving off-the-wind toward the opposite shore. She became apprehensive. "I'd better go back. My mother will be needing this cumin that I bought at the market."

"Sure if you want to." The man shifted the rudder and the boat began swinging around. "Put your head down when the sail comes around, the boom will hit you!"

Tamar stole a sidewise glance at her companion. He was quite handsome with a short, neatly trimmed beard and blue eyes that twinkled in a swarthy face. He broke into song, not ribald, just exuberant and hearty.

She obediently ducked her head. She was relieved to be going back. It had been an exciting adventure, but she dreaded explaining to her parents. However, in spite of her trepidation, nothing had happened. On the contrary, he had been courteous and considerate.

"How would you like to make one hundred denarii?" the man asked.

The question intrigued her. She remembered how excited her father had been when he made that much working in a vineyard for three months.

"How would I make one hundred denarii?"

"Go to the other side of the lake and lie with me," he said in a casual tone.

But she knew what that meant and also the consequences. It was no casual thing. She was young, but not ignorant. Her future, her very life would be at risk. The familiar shore was fast approaching. They were coming back much faster than going out because they were sailing with-the-wind. Why did she hesitate? The obvious answer was: NO. It would be moral suicide to accept his offer. "I'll go," she said. She had made her choice.

He handed her a bag full of coins. The unanticipated weight dragged it from her grip, and it slipped to the bottom of the boat where she left it. He moved the tiller and the boom swung around again. The bargain had been made. Tamar sensed that he wouldn't let her change her mind. She felt detached, compelled to follow a scenario beyond her comprehension. When they reached the opposite shore, she stepped out of the boat, still clinging to the spices she had bought at the market. She followed the man to a cave, where a mat was already spread on the floor. She removed her clothing without protest, and it was soon over. They sailed back to Capernaum in silence and he left her at the lake shore. She took the pouch of money and walked toward her home.

The sun had already slipped behind Karn Hattin when Tamar turned into the courtyard. Her mother was stirring a pot of lamb stew over an open fire, and her father was washing away the grime of a day's toil.

"Bring the cumin, child. I need to add it to the lamb stew for flavor," Adah said, holding out her hand expectantly.

Tamar had been rehearsing a story to explain her tardiness, but she had forgotten about the spices. "I must have left it in the cave."

Immediately her father responded. "What were you doing in a cave?"

She was trapped. No point in telling anything but the truth. Unembellished facts came pouring out in bold defiance.

Furiously, Diklah denounced her deed. "No decent man will marry you. Don't you know you have made a whore of yourself?"

"I don't care. Why should I slave for one man, when I can have any man in Capernaum and get rich?" Tamar retorted.

Diklah stiffened, but said no more. He entered the house and returned with her clothes. "Take your clothes and get out. You're not our daughter anymore. I should turn you over to the priests to be stoned." He dropped the bag of clothes in front of her and turned away at the import of what he had just said.

She picked up the bundle and started down the moonlit road toward Capernaum. This morning she had walked down this same road with a light step . . . the darling little girl of a doting father. Now, she was a homeless outcast . . . on a dark and forbidding road to an unknowable future. Only the light of the full moon toward which she was walking made her progress easier and gave her a glimmer of hope. The night would have been darker had the moon not shone.

It was not so in the dark and deserted streets of Capernaum. Buildings cast shadows that concealed unknown and imaginary fears. With stealth and caution Tamar felt her way to the familiar marketplace and sat down in front of the spices stall. She wrapped herself in her cloak, which had been included in the bundle her father had pitched to her in a last gesture of rejection. She didn't cry. She had made her choice, and she accepted the consequences of that choice. Tomorrow she would look for a place to live. One hundred denarii would last a long time if she could find a cheap room to rent. She felt the bulging money bag under her cloak. Somehow she gained a little comfort from having money.

Suddenly, a figure appeared out of the darkness. The brief comfort of the money bag was swept away in cold fear. Robbers had killed for less money than was in the bag.

"Don't be afraid, Tamar. I'll find you a place to stay tonight." The voice was that of the man who had taken her on the boat ride. Her terror turned to relief and cautious trust.

Confiding in him, she said, "My father made me leave home."

"I just told you I would find you a place to stay." She didn't know his name nor where they were going, but she had no choice but to follow him when he beckoned to her. They walked through Capernaum until they reached the eastern outskirts, where they came to a large house with a courtyard in front. He opened the gate and went inside.

Inside the house a lamp on a low table was burning feebly. When the man refilled the reservoir with oil, the lamp revealed a large banquet room. He lighted a candle from the lamp and beckoned for her to follow. He pulled a latch-string and a pivoted door opened inward toward the banquet room. Beyond the door, a short hallway ended at a barred door. On either side of the hall were rooms. The opening to the room on the left was covered with reeds suspended from the lintel to within a foot from the floor. Tiny bells were attached to the bottoms of the reeds. Pushing aside the reeds, they entered a room with tapestry-covered walls. A huge canopied bed tied up all the space except for a small table holding an incense tray and perfumes.

"Here is where you will entertain your guests. It will be much better than a mat in a cave," he chuckled. She saw no humor in his jest but said nothing.

Crossing to the room on the right, he flung back the crude sheet that hung over the opening. The room was as austere as the other had been ornate . . . a mat on the floor, a wash stand and a water pot. "Here is where you will sleep and wash before and after each visit," he said, emphasizing the word "wash." "Most of your guests will use that door," he said, pointing to the barred door. "Be sure to take the bars down in the morning."

They returned to the banquet hall where he set the candle on the table and left without another word. "Who was that man?" Tamar wondered. He hadn't told her his name, although he knew hers. She hadn't seen him before today, yet she had gone sailing with him, had sex with him and was now living in his house. All this in one day, a day that had destroyed her world and changed her life forever. She had left home that morning a happy, innocent child on an errand for her mother, and now she was a despised daughter, a soiled specimen of fornication . . . a hopeless outcast.

Unwittingly, she had chosen the oldest female profession.

She understood the words used by her seducer: guests, visits, and customers in the context of whoredom. Harlotry was despised by respectable people, outlawed yet tolerated by the rulers, and judging by the size of the bag in her possession, a well-paying occupation. Sleep did not come, but tears did.

When the morning light filtered through the lattice covering the high window to her room, Tamar could hear the birds chirping a happy song. After her morning ritual of bath and dressing, she unbarred the door at the end of the hall. She was rewarded with a view of a garden of fig and olive trees. As she was enjoying the view from the doorway, a man materialized from the thicket and walked toward her on the garden path. He was neat, well-dressed, with the demeanor of the ruling class.

"Are you Tamar?" he asked, not as a question, but as an assumption.

"Yes," she replied hesitantly.

"Let's see what you can do," he said, handing her five denarii. Not waiting for her to invite him in, he pushed past her and parted the reeds to the guest chamber. She was forced to accept the finality of the course her life had taken. Her first customer was waiting.

No further words were spoken. He satisfied his desires and left by the same path he had come. She went into her bedroom, bathed, perfumed and prepared for her next customer. The next customer made no more conversation than the first. Tamar perceived herself not as a person, but a safety valve to relieve repressed male sexual drives, nothing more.

Her last customer, Shealtub, was as loquacious as the other two had been taciturn. "Shealtub is my name. It means 'pig grease,' but I don't mind, it describes me," he said with a guffaw. His descriptions did fit his five-foot, four-inch frame with piled on flab, topped by a bald head that had once been covered with red hair. However, Tamar did not share his humor, even though he directed it at himself. He kept up a running conversation his entire stay.

"I'm too fat and ugly to marry, so I pay as I go," he laughed as he was leaving. His sense of humor, his incessant chatter, everything about him had so utterly repulsed Tamar that she hoped he would not come back. It was a vain hope; he became a regular customer.

She was sinking into the abyss of whoredom (no womanhood and no choices, a human thing that men used only for entertainment.) Why had she thought that all the money in the world could compensate for a situation like this? She closed the garden door.

Shortly after mid-day, there was a knock at the front gate. Tamar hastened through the front doorway, where she was confronted with a painted lady in her mid-thirties. She was wearing a skullcap on her shaved head and a faded robe that stopped at mid-calf. She stepped around Tamar and entered without being invited. "I am Oreb. I have come to instruct you in the art of harlotry," she began without salutation.

"I am Tamar." Tamar tried to be polite.

"I know who you are. You are Sether's latest recruit. He was not exaggerating; you are a fine specimen of young female beauty," Oreb said. She inspected Tamar as a farmer might inspect a prize cow, touching her breasts, thighs and hips and running her fingers through her hair. "Puberty sells. Sether tells me that you are only twelve. Beauty fades fast in this business; however, there are techniques to keep men interested into your middle age. By that time, you'll be working for me. Sether only keeps them until about twenty."

Tamar's curiosity surfaced. "Who is Sether?"

"You don't know!" Oreb exclaimed. "My dear, Sether is your master and you'd better not forget it."

"He has been very nice to me."

"He was very nice to the widow that lived here before until she couldn't pay the exorbitant rent. Then he moved her out to make it into a high-paying house of prostitution."

"What will become of the widow?"

"Who cares? You'd better listen to my instructions. You're going to need them. Right now Sether is soliciting for you, but you will need to sell yourself. Surprisingly, some men will be reluctant even after entering your house."

Oreb taught her what to do and say. Tamar doubted that she would need Oreb's advice; all of her customers had been eager. Little did she know that she would be using the advice before the day was done.

Soon after Oreb departed, there was another knock at the front gate. Who could it be, Tamar wondered, since Oreb had assured her that all customers would come to the rear through the garden? She hoped it wouldn't be another unwanted teacher like Oreb, who had charged her ten denarii for the two hours of instruction. She was pleasantly surprised to find a handsome man in his early twenties. A silk simlah and tall linen turban proclaimed him to be a wealthy merchant. Brown, friendly eyes met hers, disarming her.

"Come into the house," she invited. He entered behind her, swept the room with his eyes and came back to her with a questioning look.

"I think I may have made a mistake. My name is Adonijah and I am a wool merchant. I was informed that you made woolen clothing, but I don't see a loom."

"I'm not a weaver; whether or not you have made a mistake remains to be seen."

"I don't want to waste your time if you don't make woolen garments."

"You are not wasting my time. Perhaps I can show you something more interesting than woolen garments."

"I must leave before your husband returns," the man said, reddening at the implication of his statement.

"I don't have a husband," Tamar said impishly.

"But what do you do? No loom. No husband."

"I satisfy the desires of husbands whose wives don't."

The faint red of embarrassment became a full flush as her words sank into his understanding, and he said, "You can't mean that a beautiful, young girl like you is a practicing harlot?"

"Tell me, if I were old and ugly, would I have any customers?"

"I've made a mistake. I must be going," he said. But he didn't rise from his cushion.

"If you must go, I'll not stop you, but you are a very interesting person to talk to. Tell me about yourself. Are you married? Do you have any children?"

"Yes, I'm married. Miriam and I have one child, a boy." The statement was simple, but Tamar detected a vague hint that the marriage was not all that Adonijah had hoped for.

"Do you love your wife?" Tamar thrust the verbal sword straight to his heart.

"Of course, I love her! You don't think I would have married her if I didn't?" He arose from his cushion in anger.

"Don't be angry. Many marriages are made for other reasons than love. If they weren't, I would soon be out of business."

His anger subsided as quickly as it had erupted. They sat in silence for what seemed a long time.

When he seemed to be getting uncomfortable, she arose and said, "I would like to give it free, but my master insists on five denarii. Leave it on the stand and follow me."

He hesitated a moment, then left the money and followed her into the guest room. Eagerly she gave herself to the one man she wanted but would never have.

Night had fallen when she let him out the back entrance. For a little while, lovemaking had been a pleasure; tomorrow it would be a chore.

Monetary compensation made the routine endurable. Because her patrons were wealthy, the chest she purchased to replace the bag Sether had given her was already half full. None objected and some added to the five denarii that was the apparent accepted rate for her services.

Since respectable men were expected to be at their place of business in the afternoon and with their families at night, her afternoons were free. She went to the communal well to fill her waterpots and down to the stream to do her laundry, but her social life was nil. Women hated her and men didn't want to be seen with her in public.

One afternoon when she returned from market, Sether was counting her money. "Only five hundred more and you'll have enough to pay the rent you owe me."

"But I thought . . . ," she didn't finish.

"What did you think? That I was going to give you this house because I felt sorry for you that your father had thrown you out. Hardly. This is an ideal place for high class entertainment: a back entrance through a garden, a front entrance from a large courtyard enabling you to monitor other callers, and an ivory bed with tapestry from India. I have a lot invested in you, girl. It's time I got some money back."

"You promised me . . ."

"Plenty of money, nice clothes, whatever you want. I know what I promised you. Here is what you get." He reached into a corner and brought out a whip and with one swift movement he slammed her against a wall and beat her with just enough force to bring intense pain without leaving permanent marks. She started to scream.

"Don't scream," he said. "Someone may hear you."

She put her hands over her mouth to stifle the screams. He continued to beat her until she collapsed on the floor, whimpering and begging. Her resistance was gone. He was her master.

"You shall have nice clothes. I want you to buy the best. I want my girls to look like queens. How much money you have will depend on you. I have been soliciting for you to get you started. You can serve ten clients per day. Find them yourself. Oreb will teach you how. Shealtub will keep me informed of your progress." Without another word he was gone, taking all the money in the chest.

From the floor, Tamar arose a broken woman. Gone was her virginity, her home, her innocence and now her spirit. She was Sether's slave. He had taken the money (her sense of security) and expected her to find more customers. She waited two days for Oreb to barge in. A week ago she had not wanted to see Oreb again.

When Shealtub came for his weekly visit, she interrupted his incessant chatter. "Where does Oreb live?" she asked.

"You don't know? I'll show you." He seemed glad for the opportunity. A short distance from Tamar's house, they came to a large inn. Camels, donkeys, horses and even oxen were tied to posts, trees and walls. "You'll find her in there someplace," he said, indicating a gate opening into an enormous courtyard.

A huge pot was hanging over a wire in the center of the courtyard. Roman soldiers dressed in military attire mixed with merchants, fishermen and traders. Occasionally, a guest would take a piece of dry bread from a fold in his cloak and dip it into the pot.

When Oreb came out of the inn carrying a leg of lamb to put in the pot, Tamar hurried to her side. "Shalom, Oreb."

"Shalom, Tamar. I've been expecting you. Come inside. Shealtub told me that you needed more instructions in soliciting."

"I didn't know where you lived."

"Thought I lived in a house like yours? My dear, my clientele is different from Sether's. Local men have to be discreet. Only travelers stop at an inn. No one knows or cares what they do there. I don't have to solicit. My girls always have plenty to do."

Tamar almost bristled at the implication that those who came to her house were Sether's customers, but she remembered that she was a slave and could call nothing her own. "I need more money to pay my rent and still have enough for household and personal expenses."

Oreb smiled. "My dear, you'll never have enough to pay your rent, but if Sether wants you to solicit, you'd better solicit. Marketplace—you'll find customers there."

"That is where I met Sether."

"Of course. A good place to scout, too."

"You mean he was looking for harlots?"

"Potential harlots. No self-respecting girl would talk to a man in the marketplace."

"He was nice to me in the marketplace."

"He was nice to the widow who used to live in the house where you live until she couldn't pay the exorbitant rent. He threw her out."

"What happened to the woman?"

"Who knows. Who cares." Oreb showed no compassion, but asked for another ten denarii.

"I don't have any money."

"Sether take it all?"

Tamar nodded.

"That was two days ago. Don't lie to me. Shealtub knows how many customers you've had since."

Cowed, Tamar reluctantly gave her the ten denarii she had received from Shealtub and another customer that morning.

She went directly from the inn to the marketplace. She was looking at a cluster of grapes when a voice behind her said, "Shalom, Tamar. I've been wanting to talk to you."

Adonijah! The very sound of his voice sent pleasure to the tips of her toes.

She turned toward the voice. "Oh, Adonijah, I didn't think that I would ever see you again. How did you know me in this veil and cloak?"

"Sweet Tamar, you couldn't hide your loveliness under a tent," he said with a smile.

She had an intense desire to slip into his arms. Instead, she began the customary ritual of inquiring about the health of family members and relatives. "How is your wife?"

"She is in mourning."

"Did her mother or father die?"

"No, our little son."

"Oh, I'm so sorry. You are in mourning, too."

"Blessed are they that mourn for they shall be comforted," he said. What strange words. They sounded like a quotation from the Prophets.

"I will come to your house tonight."

"But you will be missed at your house."

"My wife doesn't want me at home. She blames me for our son's death."

"Why?"

"Because I took him with me to sell wool in Decapolis. She thinks they put a curse on him. I remonstrated with some of the Jewish brethren who tolerated swine sacrifice. The barbarians chased us out of town with stones. When we got back to Capernaum, little Andrew had a high fever. He died before morning."

"Do you believe that they put a curse on him?"

"No, I was right to oppose swine sacrifice."

"Why did he die?"

"I don't know, but I believe that someday I'll see him again."

Tamar came back to his coming to her house. "I would like for you to come to my house tonight, but are you sure it would be wise?"

"I'll be there at the twelfth hour," he said with a finality that forbade argument.

As the evening shadows lengthened, Tamar made a fire in the fireplace and prepared a simple meal. There had been a fire in the fireplace when Sether had brought her here, but she had not needed a fire since, preferring to cook outside in the courtyard. But tonight was special. She was preparing for her lover, and a fire would be romantic.

At sunset Adonijah boldly knocked at the gate. They ate the simple meal and relaxed on the cushions at the low table.

"That was a tasty and satisfying meal. Where did you learn to cook like that?" Adonijah asked.

"Didn't expect a whore to know how to do anything but make love? My mother is a good cook, and although I spent my daylight hours in the fields with my father, my mother taught me how to cook."

"Stop calling yourself a whore," he chided.

"I know what I am. So does every man in Capernaum. They know who I am, where I am, and what I can do about it: absolutely nothing," she replied with resignation.

"There is something you can do about it," Adonijah protested.

"Adonijah, you don't understand. I am Sether's slave. He is in complete control of my life." Then, beginning with her encounter with Sether at the marketplace, she left out no details of the vile affair.

"Poor, little girl. I am ashamed that I took advantage of the trap you are in. I am guilty of incest, because I regard you as a daughter."

"Adonijah, you can't be my father . . . ." She wanted him to be her lover, but the earnestness in his face told her that it would never be.

"Didn't you just say that your father said, 'You are not our daughter anymore.' You have to be somebody's daughter. Why can't you be mine?"

"All right, I'll be your pretend daughter. Will you rock me to sleep?" She snuggled up to him on a cushion and he put an arm around her shoulders. Surprisingly, she did go to sleep. He slipped out the front way, leaving her asleep in the banquet hall.

Early the next morning, he was again at her gate. There was a noticeable radiance in his face. His whole being exuded joy and excitement.

"You look like you just sold a ton of wool," Tamar said. "Come in."

"No, I want you to come with me. I have a surprise for you."

"I'm sorry, but I have guests to serve this morning, or did you forget?"

"Leave the door barred."

"I can't do that. Sether will beat me to death!"

"If you come with me, Sether won't touch you."

She looked into his eyes and saw a strong, determined will and felt safe. "I'll need my kaffiyeh."

Adonijah waited patiently in the courtyard until she reappeared wearing a veil under her headdress.

"Why are you wearing a veil?" he asked.

"You don't want your friends to know who I am," she explained.

"Take it off. I refuse to be ashamed of my daughter!"

She took it off and followed him through the gate, glad that her pretend father was not like her real father.

They walked in deserted streets that were normally crowded at this time of day with people going to and from the marketplace. The few people they met seemed not to notice an older man with a young woman following him at a discreet distance.

"I wonder why there are so few people on the streets today," Tamar remarked.

"Everybody has gone down to the lake shore to hear Jesus of Nazareth teach," Adonijah replied.

"Oh, I have heard of him, but it wouldn't do me any good to hear a holy man. I've gone too far. Decent people will never want anything to do with me."

"You are with me, and I am decent, am I not?"

"Your wife might not think so. Adultery is not considered a sin if you pay for it, but respectable men do not appear in public with a harlot."

"Before you judge me or yourself, wait until you hear Jesus of

Nazareth," he said, taking her hand as they approached the throng on the shore of Lake Galilee.

Nearing the crowd, Tamar could hear a clear and distinct voice saying, "A farmer was sowing grain in his field. As he scattered the seeds, some fell on the path and the birds found them and ate them; some fell among the stones where the soil was shallow. The plants sprouted and grew quickly, but the hot sun scorched them and they withered and died. Other seeds fell on thorn-infested soil and were choked out by the thorn plants. Those seeds that fell on deep fertile soil produced a bountiful crop—some thirty, some sixty and some a hundred times more than was sown. If you have ears to hear, listen."

Tamar easily identified with the story. She had often tried to shoo the birds away when she had gone with her father into the fields.

"No use trying to scare the birds away, Little Palm Tree, the earth on the path is packed too hard for the seeds to sprout anyway," Diklah had said.

Later, some of the plants sprouted and grew quickly, but her delight had turned to dismay when the little plants withered and died. Her mind returned to the present and she began to cry. "Oh, Adonijah, I am just like those little seeds. My life is withered and hopeless. My father named me Tamar because he hoped I would be like a fruitful palm tree and I have made a mess of my life. I . . . I . . . just wish I could start over."

"You can start over," he comforted her. "Jesus can forgive your sins and you will become a new person." He led her through the dispersing crowd, who had come to see the miracles but had no understanding of the mysterious parable and no inclination to learn. Only the twelve closest associates of Jesus were listening to his further expounding of the story. Adonijah had released her hand and slipped away without her being aware of his going.

What should she do? Those gathered around Jesus were men, but there were six or eight women in a little group apart. Normal female instinct would have her join the women, but she had been shunned by women for so long that she had no desire for their company. She boldly joined the men.

Jesus looked at her and said, "Tamar, your sins are forgiven. Don't go back to your house."

She felt a gentle hand on her shoulder. "Come, you can live with me," a woman spoke kindly to her.

"But you don't know who I am. I am Tamar, the harlot."

"You were Tamar, the harlot, but Jesus has given you new life—just as he did me. I am Mary of Magdalene. Jesus threw seven devils out of me."

"Why did Jesus tell me not to go back to my house?"

"Your house is a house of harlotry. You must never go back there."

Mary Magdalene's house was very commodious. There was an ample dining hall, a spacious upper room and several sleeping rooms that were given privacy by reed screens. Mary introduced Tamar to Joanna and Susanna. Other women came in later, making ten in all. They wore expensive clothing and jewelry. Two of the women, besides Mary the Magdalene, owned houses. They were all widows except Joanna, whose husband Chuza, worked for King Herod and Mary, wife of Cleophas, Jesus' aunt.

After the servants had cleared the dishes away from the evening meal, Joanna addressed the group of women. "Jesus and the Twelve are going to need some new clothing. They can't continue traveling around Judea and Galilee for nothing. They have expenses. I'm wondering if we women can't help out."

"I think that is an excellent idea," said Mary, the wife of Cleophas.

"Most of us have our jewelry and others have a good income from our estates. Of course, Susanna doesn't have much," Joanna continued.

"I have my two hands and a loom. If I had some wool, I could weave Jesus a new robe. I noticed the one he is wearing is threadbare," Susanna said.

"Oh," Tamar said excitedly. "I've got some wool. Adonijah paid me with wool one time. Well . . . not really; he just came to talk that time." She blushed at what she had said.

Joanna smiled. "Your past is behind you, but what you received is yours to do with as you please."

"I'll get it first thing in the morning . . . but I can't . . . go back to my house," Tamar said.

"Jesus told her not to go back to her house," Mary Magdalene explained. "It's a house of prostitution." None of the women seemed shocked by the explanation. Tamar had found acceptance.

She slept the best that night that she had slept since she was a child at home. She felt clean inside and so happy. Her sins were all forgiven. Jesus said so. It was so wonderful! He had saved her from that awful life of harlotry. She could begin again! Her heart filled with gratitude as she slipped away into blissful slumber.

"Jesus has been invited to Simon the Pharisee's house for supper," Susanna told the group of women the next morning as she wove a seamless robe for Jesus on her loom from the wool Mary Magdalene had supplied. "Where did you get this wool?" she asked Mary.

"I went over to Tamar's house and got it this morning. The priest wouldn't let me in the house, but the servants had already brought everything out of the house to burn. They will scrape the walls. Sether had leprosy. It won't be used as a house of prostitution anymore," Mary Magdalene said.

Susanna took the wool and began immediately to weave a cloak for Jesus. Without interrupting her work, she said, "Thank you for the wool, Tamar. It's very good quality and easy to work with. As I was saying, Jesus has been invited to Simon the Pharisee's house for supper. I guess the Pharisees are finally going to accept Jesus as a legitimate teacher."

"I doubt that," Joanna said. "Chuza says that the Jews say that because Jesus has not attended a recognized rabbinical school, and because he stirs up the people, he should be killed."

"But if they believed that, why would Simon invite him to supper?" Susanna asked.

"I don't know," Joanna answered.

Mary Magdalene had finished counting the money they had pooled.

"Let's take this money over to Hachilah's house," she said. "Jesus and the Twelve are staying there while they are in Capernaum."

However, they were already gone when the women arrived.

"They have gone down to the shore of Galilee," Hachilah said. "I am concerned about Jesus' health. He hardly sleeps at all. He went out into the mountains to pray last night and didn't return until the third watch. Then he and the Twelve left here at daybreak. Also, I worry about their finances; Peter and Andrew and Zebedee's sons just left their nets and followed Jesus all over Judea and Galilee. Zebedee is trying to keep the fishing business going, but he comes home exhausted every night. Hannah says that he can't do as much as he did when he was younger."

"Who is Hannah?" Tamar asked.

"Forgive me, my dear, I forgot that you are new to our group. Hannah is my sister and mother of James and John," Hachilah explained.

The women thanked Hachilah and went to look for Jesus and his disciples. They didn't tell her what they had in mind, because they knew that she would also want to share out of her meager substance. Although she fretted over her boys (she tried to mother them all, including Jesus), she really was very proud of them and was secretly glad for what they were doing. She had opened her home and fed them while they were staying in Capernaum. If it could be said that they had a headquarters, her house was it.

By the time the women had found the band of disciples, they were nearing Chorazin. They couldn't get near Jesus because of the crowd, but they found Philip and Andrew.

"Jesus just drove a demon out of a man who couldn't talk. And then he could talk. Actually he can't quit talking," Andrew laughed.

"Jesus is in a boat now," Tamar said. Jesus' voice came loud, clear and distinct across the water as though he were standing at their elbow. The words flowed from his mouth as effortlessly as a brook flowing downhill.

"We women have gathered together a bag of money to help with the expenses of the Group," Mary Magdalene told Andrew.

"I'll find Matthew. He would be the logical person to carry the money, because he had experience as a publican before he became a disciple," Andrew chuckled, then went to search for Matthew in the crowd. It was some time before he came back with Judas, instead of Matthew.

"Matthew said that he was going to be busy writing a biography of Jesus and suggested that I ask Judas to take care of the money. Judas has consented to do it, if that is acceptable with you women."

"That will be fine with us," Mary Magdalene said, turning to the others. "Don't you agree?"

They agreed and Judas of Kerioth began to carry the money bag for the group of Twelve Apostles that Jesus had chosen.

CHAPTER 7

SIMON, THE PHARISEE

The disciples were excited. Jesus had been invited to Simon the Pharisee's house for an evening meal. Jesus was the only one invited to eat, but his disciples were welcome to watch. The women came, too. It would be a treat to see how rich people lived. The dining hall was open to the outer courtyard.

"I hear he has ten servants," Philip said.

"Oh, I don't think he has that many," Andrew said, smiling at Philip's exaggeration.

At the appointed hour, Simon reclined his guests at a low, U-shaped table. He reclined himself where he could see and be seen by the spectators. Jesus reclined directly across from Simon.

Tamar had been planning all day in her mind what she would do tonight. She had found a vial of her most expensive perfume in the wool that Mary Magdalene had brought from her house. Her heart was so full of gratitude for the new life that Jesus had given her that she must express it some way. When all the Twelve had reclined at the table, Tamar recognized her opportunity. She slipped in behind Jesus, intending to pour the perfume on his feet. Suddenly, she was overcome with emotion. She couldn't hold back the tears. They ran down her cheeks and splashed on Jesus' feet. Her hair, which grew to her waist, became a convenient towel to wipe away the tears from his feet.

Simon saw Tamar come in. He knew who she was, but he had no idea why she was here. He was about to order her out because he didn't want her soliciting his guests. When she knelt behind Jesus, he thought, "If he really is a prophet, he will know what kind of woman she is." His flesh crawled as she uncovered Jesus' feet. Jesus was allowing her to kiss his feet! The nerve of that woman, trying to solicit his honored guest right in his own home. He was ready to call his servants and have them throw her out.

"Simon." Jesus had to call out Simon's name to get his attention, so intently had he been watching Tamar. "I have something to say to you."

"I'm listening, teacher," Simon answered. He wondered how Jesus was going to explain allowing a harlot to kiss his feet.

"A certain rich man loaned money to two people: five thousand denarii to one and five hundred to the other. But neither of them could pay him back, so he kindly forgave them both, letting them keep the money. Which do you suppose loved him most after that?"

"I suppose the one who owed him the most," Simon answered.

"Correct," Jesus agreed. Then he turned to Tamar and said, "See this woman kneeling here. When I entered your house, you didn't offer me water to wash the dust off my feet, but she has washed them with her tears and wiped them with her hair. You didn't give me a greeting kiss on the cheek, but she has kissed my feet. You didn't anoint my head with oil, but she has anointed my feet with costly perfume. Therefore, her sins, which are many, are forgiven. She has shown much love for me. Those who have been forgiven little, show little love."

Then, turning to Tamar, he said, "Your sins are forgiven."

The other Pharisees whom Simon had invited began whispering among themselves, "Who does this man think he is, forgiving sins? Only God can forgive sins."

Again Jesus said to Tamar, "Your faith has saved you. Go in peace."

She went out with a heart full of joy and a mouth full of praise to God.

CHAPTER 8

STORM

It was early morning. Judas was feeling good about himself. Jesus had talked to him for quite some time last night after they left Simon's house.

"I'm glad the women gave us some money. That will make them so happy. Now we will have something to give to the poor," Jesus had said. "I am also glad that they have chosen you to take care of the money. I am sure that you will keep an accurate record of what we receive and what we give. You need to guard it closely so that no one will steal from it."

Judas appreciated Jesus' confidence in him. Jesus was so warm and friendly. One couldn't help liking him. He wondered about that Pharisee, though. Jesus had put him down in front of his friends. Judas knew that outfit. The Pharisees were so proud. They didn't think they should pay taxes like ordinary folks. He remembered how they hated him when he collected from them. They muttered under their breath, but they didn't dare say anything aloud because there was always a Roman soldier nearby. Judas laughed to himself. They even spat at him when the soldier wasn't looking. But there hadn't been any Roman soldier last night. Judas hadn't understood about the woman's sins being forgiven. He didn't know her. Jesus said that she was a harlot, but surely Jesus didn't believe that God would forgive a harlot. Well, anyway, Jesus had put Simon in his place, and that gave Judas satisfaction.

They went out to the lake shore again that morning. Already a crowd was gathered and more were coming. They came hobbling on homemade crutches, some on stretchers and others being helped by friends. One boy had an open sore that smelled like dead rats. Judas gagged as he passed by. One man was dragging one leg, which was swollen so large that only his toes projected beyond his foot, giving it the appearance of an elephant's leg. Women were carrying babies with tiny arms and legs but stomachs like melons. Where did they all come from? Here was a man being led by two others. His eyelids were curved in toward the cornea. Constant irritation gave the cornea a frosted appearance. The man grimaced in pain as the eyelashes dug into his eyeballs. It was a terrible time for humanity. Every imaginable disease and no cure. The physicians knew very little about treating illness. Sometimes the patient's own body healed itself and the physician took credit. Often the cure only worsened the condition. The lucky ones were those who contracted some fatal disease that brought death quickly. The poor could not afford what little medical knowledge was available. And so they came to Jesus. Relatives came to help them get there.

And there was a crowd of spectators who had come to be entertained by the miracles. They didn't really care about the sufferers, but they were fascinated by the miracles. And finally, there were the scribes and Pharisees who came to criticize. They didn't care about the sick and the suffering, nor the miracles, but they hoped to trap Jesus in misinterpretation of the Law in order to discredit him with the people.

Jesus spent all morning healing people. The noonday sun was hot. The breeze coming from the lake was all that made it bearable, but the crowd stayed on, not seeming to mind the heat. Finally, the last cripple hobbled up. Jesus healed him, and he went off through the crowd laughing and praising God.

Jesus got into an empty fishing boat that had been pulled up on the beach. He pushed it out a little way from the shore and anchored it. With the breeze behind him and the water to amplify his voice, he spent the rest of the day teaching.

Judas stayed on shore. He didn't understand parables, and even though Jesus later explained it all privately, it was still too deep for him. He was glad when the sun sank behind the western mountains. The sky was red where the sun was setting. The breeze from the lake had stopped, and the cooler part of the day began. The crowd dispersed.

"Let us go over to the other side of the lake," Jesus said. The Twelve waded out to the boat and climbed in. Jesus was sitting at the rear of the boat. Although the sun had disappeared behind the mountains in the west, the beams still glistened on the snows of Mount Hermon to the north. Meanwhile, dark clouds began to build above the western mountains.

"Storm's brewing," James said.

"Maybe we can beat it," Andrew added.

"I've seen them come over those mountains pretty fast," replied James.

Darkness was falling fast, and they deemed it wise to cross the lake as quickly as they could. Since there was no wind, they had no choice but to row. All took turns. Peter, James, John and Andrew made every stroke count. Lifelong experience, plus peak physical condition made it seem effortless for them. When it came Judas' turn, his unfamiliarity with boats and lack of hard physical labor made it difficult for him. There were four oars and they worked in teams of two. Judas was splashing and puffing and causing the boat to go off course.

"Try to pull at the same time as Matthew does, Judas," Peter explained. "Here, let me show you. Bend forward. Lower the oar into the water. Pull back. Raise the oar. Bend forward again."

Judas tried, but what was second nature to Peter was an awesome task for him. He didn't say anything, but inwardly he was seething. It looked to him like Jesus could take a turn instead of sleeping. Just then the storm hit with all its fury. The boat tipped to one side.

"Everybody lean the other way!" Peter shouted. They did and the boat righted itself, but not before quite a bit of water had run into it.

"Row into the wind!" Peter yelled. He grabbed the oar out of Judas' hand. Andrew, James and John took the other three oars and soon brought the boat around into the wind.

"Judas, get that bucket and start bailing," Peter commanded.

Judas inwardly raged, but he was too scared to do anything but obey. They rowed as hard as they could, but it was hopeless. More and more water came into the boat as the waves broke over the prow.

"Do you think we ought to awaken Jesus?" Thomas asked.

"Not unless we have to," John said. "He needs his rest. We've been out in storms before."

"I've never seen a storm this bad before and neither have you," James yelled. "Dad would never have let us leave shore with clouds coming over the mountains like that."

"But we had no idea it was going to storm!" John yelled back.

"I was uneasy when the wind died down at sunset and those clouds rose over the tops of the mountains," Peter said.

Judas had heard enough. These men were experienced fishermen and they were afraid. He couldn't understand how Jesus could sleep during all this turmoil. So he was going to wake him. It had been his idea to cross the lake tonight. He made his way to the sleeping form.

Shaking him, he yelled irritably, "Teacher, why don't you care that we are all about to drown?"

Jesus arose and made his way to the bow of the boat. The men were still straining at the oars.

Facing into the wind, he commanded, "Stop it! Be still!"

One moment there had been a fierce, howling and tearing wind with huge waves breaking over the helpless boat. Now the moon was shining and the clouds were gone; only a gentle breeze remained. Except for the water in the bottom of the boat, there was no evidence that there had ever been a storm. Judas was more afraid than he had been before. What kind of man was Jesus, anyway? He had scolded the wind just as one would a slave, and it had obeyed him instantly. It was uncanny. It was unnatural. It was scary.

"What were you afraid of?" Jesus asked. "Where is your faith?"

Judas couldn't understand what faith had to do with it. He resumed dipping the water out of the boat. The others bowed before Jesus and said, "Truly, you are the Son of God." Judas continued to bail water. He didn't know what else to do. He liked Jesus, but he didn't believe that he was the Son of God.

After a short period of homage, Peter said to Judas, "I'll dip. You can help Matthew with the oars."

Judas was glad to take his turn now. That which seemed to be such a struggle before became easier. He seemed to catch the rhythm, and he and Matthew pulled in time with each other.

The bottom of the boat grated ashore. The shore was entirely different from the gentle, sloping, sandy shore of Capernaum. A steep bluff ran at right angles to the lake, ending at the lake itself. The water was deep there. They had landed just north of the bluff. The face of the bluff was carved with burial caves.

A human figure emerged from one of the caves and rushed toward them, screaming as he came. Judas felt terror gripping him. He wanted to run from that horrible thing from hell. Jesus stood calmly waiting for the creature's approach. The man fell at Jesus' feet moaning.

"Come out, you evil spirit," Jesus commanded. The man uttered such a tortured, hopeless, horrible scream that Judas wished he could close his ears.

"What are you going to do to us, Jesus, Son of the most high God? Are you going to torture us before the appointed time?" The man cried out in fear. He was actually afraid of Jesus.

"What is you name?" Jesus asked, seemingly speaking to someone other than the man.

"My name is Legion. There are many of us here." The man was speaking, but it sounded as many voices in unison. "Please don't put us into the pit. Let us go into those hogs up there." By the light of the early dawn Judas could see two or three hogs rooting around on the top of the bluff.

"Go!" Jesus commanded. Suddenly, the whole herd began squealing and rushed headlong over the cliff into the lake. Because the water was deep and the cliff was rocky and steep, the hogs couldn't get a foothold, and they all drowned.

Jesus removed his outer robe and put it on Legion, who was nearly naked.

It was now daylight and the herdsmen appeared at the top of the bluff to see what was going on. Seeing the hogs in the water, they ran back to Gergasa with the news. The whole village came out and stood around talking among themselves. Finally, two of the village elders came over and said, "We don't know who you are, nor where you came from, but if you are responsible for drowning those hogs, we want you to leave. We know you Jews say that swine are unclean, but they are our living. Please, just go away and leave us alone," they begged.

"I'm not responsible for what happened to the hogs. The devils caused it, but if you want me to go, we will leave at once. I don't want to stay where I'm not wanted," Jesus said. They returned to the boat to leave.

"May I go with you?" Legion asked.

"No, you go home to your family and friends and tell them what wonderful things God has done for you and how merciful he has been," Jesus told him. Legion stood on the shore and waved as long as he could see the boat.

Peter raised a small sail making it unnecessary to row, and Judas sat in the stern, where Jesus had slept, pondering all that had happened the previous night. Just what kind of man was Jesus? He wasn't afraid of anything. He didn't have to be afraid. He could speak to the forces of nature and they obeyed him. What a king a man like that would make! If he could stop a storm, he could cause a storm and scatter his enemies. When the fields needed rain, he could command the clouds and it would rain, and he could keep the rain away in the barley harvest. He had thrown those devils out of Legion. Judas had seen people possessed with demons, but never as bad as poor Legion. Judas shuddered as he remembered the horrible scream and that ghastly apparition from the grave that greeted them at the Gerasene shore.

He was glad to be returning to Capernaum. He even welcomed the sight of the eager crowd on the friendlier Galilean shore, a sandy beach, not forbidding rocks and cliffs. The women were the first to meet them as the boat slid gently upon the sandy beach.

"Oh, Jesus, where is your cloak?" Mary Magdalene asked.

"Don't worry, I made you a new one," Joanna said, not waiting for Jesus to answer Mary's question.

"Thank you so much, Joanna. Not many seamstresses can make a garment without a seam." Jesus noticed her skill in expressing his thanks.

Jesus didn't stay at the lakeshore, but went toward the city. Judas was glad to keep moving. He often grew impatient with listening to Jesus teach, preferring to see miracles.

CHAPTER 9

JAIRUS

Jairus was worried about his daughter, Taphath. She had been listless for two weeks, but yesterday she vomited all day and her face was flushed with fever. The physician had come and given her medicine, but she vomited it, too. He and her mother had taken turns bathing her forehead with water. All last night she had moaned and tossed. At daybreak, she had started holding her stomach and screaming, "Oh, Abba, it hurts so bad!"

To avoid seeing her suffering, Jairus went out into the courtyard, but he could still hear her screams.

"Jesus of Nazareth is coming into the city!" a slave called excitedly.

"Abigail!" Jairus called to his wife, and she came out into the courtyard. "I am going to ask Jesus of Nazareth to come and heal Taphath."

"But you are apt to lose your job. The chief priest is saying that anyone having anything to do with Jesus of Nazareth will be thrown out of the synagogue," Abigail protested.

"Taphath is going to die if we don't do something," Jairus said. The girl was no longer screaming, just gasping the labored breathing of the dying.

Jairus hurried to find Jesus. He had met Jesus at another time and had invited him to speak in the synagogue where he was director. He liked to encourage young rabbis. Of course, that was before Jesus had become such a controversial figure by throwing out demons, healing lepers. Rumors were that he even raised the dead. His teaching had been very interesting, with authority, and not as the scribes and Pharisees from Jerusalem. He had to ask them to teach out of loyalty to the law, but they were so boring. They were always quoting some obscure rabbi that he had never heard of. It seemed to him that they made the Law say whatever they wanted it to say.

Last Sabbath Jairus had asked a rabbi from Jerusalem to teach. The rabbi had said that this upstart from Nazareth was performing miracles by the power of Beelzebub. Jairus didn't believe it, and as long as he was the synagogue director, Jesus was welcome to teach there. For that matter, Jesus seemed to prefer to teach at the lakeshore. The crowds couldn't get into the synagogue anyway.

Jesus was his last and only hope for Taphath, his only daughter, and his love caused him to dote on her. She was almost old enough to be given in marriage. He had been expecting Jonathon's son, Benjamin, to ask for her hand in marriage. He and Jonathon had discussed the subject, but they wanted it to be the young people's decision.

On his way out of the city, Jairus met the throng of people following Jesus into the city. He rushed up to Jesus and poured out his agony.

"Don't worry, she'll be all right," Jesus said. They started toward Jairus' home at a maddeningly slow pace. Jairus wanted to break into a run, but he knew nothing could be done without Jesus. It seemed that he could crawl as fast as they were moving. Jesus stopped! Oh, no! Didn't he realize that every second Taphath was fighting for her next breath? It was hard to rest his faith in Jesus when Taphath's life was ebbing away.

*   *   *

Esther dragged herself out of bed that morning. It was no better. She was still bleeding. She was so discouraged. She had spent the last of her savings last week. They had told her about a doctor in Cana. She had walked all the way. In her weakened condition, she had to stop to rest many times. The doctor had given her some foul-tasting medicine. If the medicine had been as effective as the taste was vile, she would have been well by now. But she was the same as she had been for twelve years. Why had she been born a woman?

Someone was knocking at her gate. "Rebecca, it is so good to see you. You look positively radiant," Esther said, greeting her friend and neighbor.

"Esther, get your kaffiyeh. I want you to see Jesus of Nazareth," Rebecca said.

"Rebecca, I don't think I can make it. That trip to Cana made me worse instead of better."

"Come on, I'll help you. Jesus is coming into the city today. I know he can cure you if we can get you there."

Esther didn't protest. She had heard about Jesus' miracles. She had tried to reach him before when he was in Capernaum, but there had been so many people that she couldn't get to where Jesus was. Also, the Law considered anyone in her condition unclean.

Rebecca helped her, and they found the crowd just outside the city gates. It was an even larger crowd than before. She couldn't see Jesus, much less get close enough for him to heal her. As the crowd moved slowly past, she had an idea. She would crawl in behind him and touch the hem of his cloak and be healed without anyone knowing she was unclean. She was making progress, worming her way through the press, until a man stepped on her hand.

"What are you doing down there on the ground?" he asked, but she didn't answer.

Just a few more feet and she could touch the garment that had been so lovingly woven by Joanna. (Was there magic in that robe?) Just a few more feet . . . the dirt, the heat and the odor were all forgotten as she reached out and touched the hem. A surge of strength and warmth coursed through her body, and she knew she had been healed.

"Who touched me?" Jesus asked. The crowd came to a halt. Esther's face flushed. She had thought that he would be unaware of her touch, but now she was exposed to the public.

"All these people pressing around you and you ask, 'Who touched me?'" said Peter.

Jesus turned and looked down at Esther. The words came tumbling out of her mouth. "I've been sick for so long . . . I thought if I could just touch . . . your clothes . . . and I am healed!"

She looked up into Jesus' smiling face and heard, "Daughter, your faith has made you well. Go in peace, healed of your disease."

*   *   *

Jairus' heart sank as he recognized the messengers from his home. "No use bothering the Teacher anymore. Taphath is dead," they said.

The worst had happened. Even without the delay, Jesus couldn't have reached his home before Taphath had died. He should have come yesterday, he had known that she was awfully sick. Grief took hold of him as he started back with the messengers.

"Wait! Don't be afraid. Just trust me," Jesus was calling to him. Only the Twelve followed Jesus. Jairus was glad that Jesus was going to be with him when he first saw his dead daughter.

The wailing of the hired mourners reached their ears as they approached the house. How could they know? He himself had only learned of Taphath's death. He knew he shouldn't, but he wished they hadn't come so soon. They were just like vultures, waiting for someone to die so they could get paid for mourning.

Jesus told his disciples to wait outside. Only James, John and Peter went inside with him. Judas felt left out, and at the same time he was relieved. He had a hard time coping with death, especially since his sister had been the same age as Taphath when she had died. Still, he resented those three privileged ones being allowed firsthand knowledge of important events. Peter later gave a detailed account of what had transpired in the house.

Upon entering the house, Jesus raised his voice above the din. "Why all this shrieking and moaning? The child is not dead, she is only asleep."

They were momentarily shocked into silence until a woman spoke in defiance. "What do you know about it? You weren't here when she breathed her last breath. I've been in the mourning business for ten years, and I have never seen anyone deader than that girl is." The other women laughed at the grisly joke.

"You may leave now," Jesus said coldly. The mourners said no more, but quietly filed out.

After that, Jesus went with Jairus and Abigail into the little room where Taphath lay. James, John and Peter followed. She was so still. Jairus started sobbing, great heaving, shaking, body-wrenching sobs. Taphath had been fighting for every breath when he left. Now, it was all over.

Jesus took her by the hand and said gently, "Get up little girl."

Taphath opened her eyes and Jesus took her by the hand and lifted her from the mat where she had lain, and she stood before them all . . . very much alive!

"Give her something to eat," Jesus commanded.

Jairus, now crying for joy, scooped her into his arms.

"Why are you crying, Abba? I'm all right," the little girl said.

The other disciples all crowded around Peter, James and John when they came back outside.

"What happened in there?" Thomas asked.

James related the miracle, but Judas would have rather seen it for himself.

CHAPTER 10

NAZARETH

It seemed to Judas that he had barely slept when Jesus roused the disciples for another day.

"Up, let us be going. There are only twelve hours in a day," he was saying cheerily.

Where does that man get all his energy, Judas wondered to himself. The only time Jesus had shown any weariness was the night of the storm. Only a few streaks of pre-dawn light announced the day as they left the city.

"Why do we need to start so early?" Judas asked Thomas.

"We are going to Nazareth today, and it's a long day's journey. Then, too, we have to leave before the crowd starts to come, or we would never get away from Capernaum."

"Nazareth is Jesus' hometown, isn't it?"

"Yes, but they tried to throw him over a cliff the last time he was there."

"Why would they want to do that? I would think they would be proud of a local man who had become popular in Capernaum and all the other cities in Galilee."

"I don't know why they tried to kill him, but if somebody treated me the way they did him, I would never go back," concluded Thomas.

They arrived at Cana about the tenth hour. They were very tired and hoped that Jesus would stay in Cana overnight and continue to Nazareth the next day, but he pressed on to Nazareth, arriving at sunset.

He stopped at Rachel's home, but her husband was surly. "You

68

needn't think that I am going to feed that gang of crackpots that wander around the country begging off honest, hard-working folks," he said. The fact that Joseph, Jesus' earthly father, had died and as the eldest son Jesus should have inherited the carpenter shop and the income thereof did not enter his thinking.

Jesus said nothing but went on to the home of Leah, his other sister. In reply to his asking for overnight accommodations, she said, "I'm sorry, but the Sabbath has already begun and I can't prepare any food."

Because the Sabbath law could not be broken to feed her own flesh and blood brother, they were forced to sleep in the street with nothing to eat. The next day they went to the synagogue. Jesus was invited to teach and began to expound the scriptures with wisdom and authority.

Judas heard muttered comments from a gray-headed man in the congregation. "Who does he think he is? He is only the son of Joseph, the carpenter."

"Joseph? Isn't he the one that married that girl he was betrothed to even after she was found pregnant? No telling who this man, Jesus', real father is," his companion said.

A third man who was seated behind them muttered, "His sisters live right here in town, but they won't have anything to do with him."

"I wouldn't want to have anything to do with a bastard brother either," the gray-headed man said.

When Jesus finished speaking, he laid his hands on a few sick people who had come to the synagogue that day, but in comparison to the crowds at Capernaum, this group was only a token.

Jesus seemed almost puzzled by the lack of response. At last he said, "A prophet is honored everywhere except in his hometown and among his relatives and his own family."

Judas felt sorry for him. A long day's march yesterday, a short night's rest in the street with no supper or breakfast and now, rejection by those who should have received him gladly. The one place where, logically, he should have a hero's welcome didn't want him.

No need to stay any longer in Nazareth. Back to Capernaum.

Not a welcome journey for thirteen weary travelers who had eaten nothing and had slept in the street. When they reached the outskirts of Nazareth, they met a big, black-bearded man riding a donkey. Suddenly, he dismounted and threw his arms around Jesus.

"Jesus!" he exclaimed. "I haven't seen you since we were kids. Remember that time we went down to Jerusalem and you got lost and it was three days before your parents found you?"

"Of course, I remember, Joezer. We both took our bar mitzvah that year."

"I'm afraid it did me no good. I'm just an old sinner. I make armor for the Roman soldiers. It pays good, but it got me thrown out of the synagogue."

Jesus smiled an understanding smile.

"Why are we standing here in the hot sun? Let's go back to my place and kill a fatted calf," Joezer said, mounting his donkey and leading the way. He turned off the road into a grove of trees. As they entered, they came to a compound. Joezer's was the largest building, but there were five other buildings with shops attached. A coppersmith was hammering on a shield, and a tanner was smoothing leather.

"Does it offend you to see people working on the Sabbath?" Joezer asked. "I don't require them to work on the Sabbath, but I pay them for the shields and harnesses when they are finished. If they want to work on the Sabbath to finish their work, I pay them. People who work for me are shunned by the Nazarenes, so they live right here on the compound.

"You may sit under the pavilion while I make supper arrangements. Help yourself to the fruit while you wait." He swept his arm toward a low table in the pavilion laden with grapes, pomegranates, figs and olives. A slave came and washed their hands and feet and anointed their heads. Soon, they were ushered into a great banquet hall where they were served veal, vegetables, herbs and fruit. They ate with an eagerness that pleased their host. Afterward, they were shown a large guest chamber where they slept. The next morning Joezer again fed them before they started on their journey to Capernaum.

A discussion arose about Joezer's violation of the Sabbath laws. James said, "I wonder if we should have eaten with him after we found out that those hired servants were working on the Sabbath."

"But he told us that they weren't required to do it. They just did it to make more money," Bartholomew said.

"They were his servants. He could have forbidden them," James continued.

"I don't know about you, but I was so hungry that I couldn't have gone another step," Judas said. "I'm glad that somebody in Nazareth was kind enough to give us something to eat."

Up to this point Jesus had said nothing, but now he said, "Joezer is a boyhood friend who still is. He that is not against us is for us."

They continued on in silence for the most part and reached Cana about noon. No one seemed to recognize them. Aside from a few curious onlookers, the villagers ignored them. It was as though a miracle had never occurred. They took the road toward Capernaum.

CHAPTER 11

FIRST KINGDOM CAMPAIGN

The sun hovered above Karn Hattin as they approached
Capernaum. Instead of continuing to the city, Jesus turned toward
the mountain on which he had outlined the Kingdom principles.
They found a small cave nearby and set up a camp for the night.

The following morning Jesus sat down on the same stone from
which he had taught the multitude in the beginning of his ministry.
He motioned them to be seated. Judas was not enthusiastic, another
boring day of teaching.

"I'm going to send you out to announce the Kingdom of Heaven
is near. Don't go to the Gentiles or the Samaritans, only to the
people of Israel, God's lost sheep. Heal the sick, cure the lepers,
raise the dead and exorcise demons. Give as freely as you have
received. Don't take any money with you. Don't even carry a
kophinos or a staff, for those you help should feed and care for
your needs. Whenever you enter a city or village, search for a godly
man and stay in his home until you leave for the next town. When
you ask permission to stay, be friendly and courteous, and if it
turns out to be a godly home, give it your blessings. If not, keep
the blessings. Any town that will not receive you, shake off the
dust from your feet as you leave. Truly, the wicked cities of Sodom
and Gomorrah will be better off at the Judgment Day than that
town. I am sending you out as sheep among wolves. Be as wary as
serpents and as harmless as doves. But beware! For you will be
arrested and tried and whipped in the synagogues. Yes, and you
must stand trial before governors and kings for my sake. This will
be your opportunity to tell them about me, yes, to witness to the

world. When you are arrested, don't worry and try to rehearse beforehand what to say, for you will be given the right words at the right time. For you won't be speaking, it will be the spirit of your heavenly Father speaking through you. Brother shall betray brother to death, and fathers shall betray their own children, and children shall turn against their parents. Everybody will hate you because you are mine. Those who hold out to the end shall be saved. When you are persecuted in one town, run to the next. I will return before you have reached all of them."

Jesus said many other things, but Judas' mind was occupied with what Jesus had already said. At least they were getting somewhere. They were going to campaign for the new kingdom.

Judas would have liked for Matthew to have been his traveling companion, but instead he was selected by Simon, the Zealot. Simon was excited and enthusiastic about their journey.

"We can go down to Judea, where we both grew up," he said.

"I wish Jesus would have let us bring some money along," Judas complained.

"Well, if we had brought money, we would get beaten and robbed. Two people are no match for robbers," Simon replied.

"I guess you are right," Judas said. He remembered the battered condition of some of the wealthy traders who had been brought into his Uncle Jesher's inn in Jericho. "But we may get robbed anyway."

"Judas, they can't rob you of something you don't have. Robbers can spot a money bag a mile away. Did you ever hear of a poor man being robbed?"

The two were getting hungry. They hadn't eaten anything since they left the mountain that morning. Jesus apparently had ground meal and baked the cakes before dawn because he had fed them at sunrise and sent them on their way. They had passed through Capernaum, around the head of Lake Galilee, and now at sunset they were on their way, on the east side of Jordan, toward Judea.

As they rounded a curve in the road, they came upon a trading caravan that had stopped for the night. Judas was frightened. He hoped that they could pass by without being seen, but it didn't happen. A big, burly, menacing-looking man stepped out into the road in front of them.

"Simon!" he exclaimed and threw his arms around Simon's waist and kissed him on both cheeks.

"Gehazi!" Simon cried, returning the kiss. "Judas, this is my brother, Gehazi," Simon said.

Judas was immediately swallowed in a bear hug. "A friend of my brother is a friend of mine!" Gehazi exclaimed.

After the usual inquiries about the health of each other's families, Gehazi wanted to know about Simon's activities. "We haven't heard anything about you since you joined up with the Nazarene."

"We are proclaiming the new Kingdom of Heaven," Simon said.

"Simon! Simon! You are always involved in some kind of political scheme. You're going to get yourself in real trouble one of these days. The Romans won't stand for any sort of government that is a threat to Caesar."

"Gehazi, you have never seen anyone like Jesus. He can heal sick folks, he can stop storms, he can exorcise demons, he can even raise the dead."

"I'm sure he is an amazing person. I've heard about him, but I know the Romans. They won't hesitate to wipe out your little band before breakfast if they think that you are going to cause trouble. Anyway, you are going to stay with us tonight," Gehazi said.

"We have time to get to Bethabara tonight," Simon said.

"I won't hear of it. Do you think I would let my own brother go without food and a place to stay tonight?"

Simon didn't protest anymore and Judas was glad. He ate heartily. They didn't often have this good a meal when they were traveling with Jesus. Gehazi was a wealthy merchant on his way north to Capernaum to sell silk and purple and perfume. He had six camels to carry his merchandise, horses for his adult family members, plus five armed horsemen for protection from robbers.

When Simon and Judas awakened the next morning, Gehazi and his caravan were already gone. "Gehazi just folds his tent and silently steals away," Simon joked.

"How does he do it?" Judas asked. "All those camels and horses would surely have made some noise."

"I don't know. Even when we were kids, he could be standing right beside me and suddenly he would be gone and I wouldn't know where or when."

"Let's be going to Bethabara." Judas was not thrilled by the prospect, but if he were going to do something, pleasant or unpleasant, he wanted to get started. As they approached the city, they met a stooped-shouldered man coming out of the city leading a donkey laden with tillage tools. Judas asked him about a place to stay.

"You'll be staying with Berechiah. He has been expecting you," the man said. "He lives in the third house beyond the gate."

Judas wondered how anyone could have known they were coming since it was only yesterday that Jesus had commissioned them.

They thanked the man and went on into the city. They knocked at the gate of the courtyard of the third house. There was a virtual explosion of children followed by a middle-aged, portly, balding man with a sprinkling of gray in his beard.

"You are the apostles of Jesus of Nazareth, aren't you?" Berechiah said, as if he were expecting them.

"Yes," said Judas. "But how did you know?"

"Gehazi is not a believer, but one of his horsemen is. He told me that you camped with Gehazi last night," Berechiah explained. "You will stay at my home while you are in Bethabara. Natasha has already prepared bread and milk for the morning meal."

While they were eating, the courtyard was filling with people. Some were on makeshift crutches. One man was blind, being led by a friend. Judas was puzzled. Where had all these people come from? Were they Berechiah's relatives? If so, he made no effort to introduce them. He seemed as puzzled as Judas. Judas looked at Simon, who was grinning.

"This is what we came for," he said. "Let's get started."

"You mean we are supposed to heal these folks?" Judas' heart pounded.

"That's right. This is what Jesus told us to do."

Judas had heard Jesus' instructions, he had even anticipated the campaign with some eagerness, to relieve boredom. He had been eager to start building the kingdom; but this, well, it just wasn't what he had expected. He was repelled by the ugly, open sores, by the sad, hopeless expressions on each face, by the overpowering, nauseating odor.

Simon began to tell the gathering about the Kingdom of Heaven and about Jesus in whose name they had come. He told them that he and Judas had been given the power to heal them. A glimmer of hope began to shine in their eyes.

Then Simon started laying hands on the sick and they were healed. Judas wanted to get away, to hide, to run. Instead, he timidly reached out to touch a little boy whose arm was twisted grotesquely. The little fellow looked up expectantly.

Judas couldn't believe that words were coming out of his mouth. "In the name of Jesus of Nazareth, be healed." Before his eyes the arm was straightened and as strong as the other arm. He had healed the boy. Yet he hadn't. The words that he had spoken just slipped out. It was as though some power beyond and above himself had used his lips and hands.

When all those in the courtyard had been healed, Simon and Judas found themselves completely exhausted. After they had rested a few minutes, Simon was eager to begin again.

"Let's go down to the marketplace and preach some more. This is great. Even the devils come out when we command them in Jesus' name."

Judas did not share Simon's enthusiasm, but because he knew that part of politics was to inform as many as possible, he went along without showing any reluctance, although he doubted that they would be heard above the din of the agora.

Every city and town had a marketplace, or agora. Wholesale and retail were meaningless terms. Every man sold his own wares.

He always asked a ridiculously high price. The buyer in turn offered a ridiculously low price for what he called inferior goods. They would trade insults for fifteen or twenty minutes. After a shouting match that would seem about to break into violence at any moment, a price was agreed upon that was somewhere between that asked and that offered. The transaction was completed with each complaining of the other cheating. Once out of earshot of the other, each man would brag about having bested the other in bargaining.

But it was not as Judas expected. As soon as they started down toward the marketplace, people followed them. The farther they went, the larger the crowd. Long before they reached the marketplace, people came streaming from that direction. Those who had been healed had broadcast the news and Judas and Simon never reached the marketplace.

Simon began immediately to heal those who had come first. Judas was again hesitant to begin. A little boy limped over to him and said, "Teacher, would you heal me? Some of us boys were playing on the housetop and I fell off and broke my leg."

The leg had healed grotesquely. It looked as though it had been healed a year, but it had grown back terribly twisted.

"Didn't your parents take you to a doctor?" Judas inquired. It was doubtful that it could have been set, since both bones were broken.

"Au, they were too poor to take me to a doctor. Besides, I can go up to the temple and beg now," the boy replied.

"You don't want to be a beggar?" Judas asked, stalling.

"No, I want to run and play with the other boys. Please, mister, heal me!" the boy pleaded. There didn't seem to be any doubt in his mind that Judas could do it. Judas could stall no longer. A cluster of people was looking his way. Concentrating all of his attention on the boy and the crippled leg, yet yielding to a mysterious force that he had experienced that morning, he said, "In the name of Jesus of Nazareth, be healed." He was afraid nothing would happen, but something did happen. The leg straightened itself as straight as the other. The boy threw his arms around Judas and then ran off through the crowd whooping and yelling with childhood exuberance.

There was a momentary lull in the hubbub of the crowd and then a man exclaimed, "He can heal, too!"

Those who had been watching to see what was happening crowded around Judas. By the ninth hour Judas and Simon had healed all those who had come for healing. The crowd began to drift away.

"Wait!" Simon cried. "I want to tell you about the Kingdom of Heaven. You don't have to be wealthy to be a citizen of this kingdom. You will inherit the earth if you are meek. If you want to be righteous, you will be righteous. If you are pure in heart, you will see God. You won't have to worry about anything because God will take care of you just like He takes care of the birds." Simon went on to explain all that Jesus had taught on the mountain. Judas was willing to let Simon do all the preaching. He couldn't remember very much of it, and he hadn't understood what he did remember. There was a lot of enthusiasm among those who heard, especially those who had been healed. However, when they learned that they were disciples of Jesus of Nazareth and would be persecuted, their enthusiasm waned.

When the sun was setting and the crowd dispersed, Judas and Simon went back to Berechiah's house. "I'm exhausted," Simon said. "It seemed every time I healed somebody, I would get weak."

"Me too," Judas answered. "That must have been how Jesus knew that woman had touched his clothes on the way to Jairus' house."

"I'm more tired than when we walk all day."

"So am I. I hope Berechiah's wife has supper prepared. I'm hungry."

Natasha did have a good meal prepared for them. After Berechiah had recited the blessing, they ate greedily, trying to observe etiquette expected of guests but overwhelmed with hunger. Berechiah smiled at their feeble efforts to be polite. He was delighted with the gusto with which his guests ate his humble food. He was a good host. When they had finished, they retired to the courtyard and Natasha and the children had a meager meal on the remnants.

"Is there a solitary place near here where we can go pray?" Simon inquired of Berechiah.

"Well, you could go out to the mountains, but the gate is shut and you couldn't get back in even if the gatekeeper let you. Why don't you go up on the housetop? It is quiet up there and no one will disturb you," Berechiah said.

"Then that is where we will go," Simon replied. "Come on, Judas, let's go pray." But Judas had wrapped his cloak around himself and was already asleep on the cobblestones of the courtyard.

Natasha and her daughter had already baked corn cakes, and were grinding more meal when the two disciples awakened at daybreak. Berechiah came out of the house and greeted them. "How long will you be staying in Bethabara?" he asked.

"We are leaving this morning," Simon answered. "We need to go to all the cities in Perea."

"Leaving so soon? I was hoping you would stay many days. I am afraid you may have trouble in Perea," Berechiah warned. "Since King Herod arrested John the Baptist, people are afraid of preachers."

"All I know is the impression I received when I prayed last night," Simon replied.

Judas followed Simon out through the city gate rather sullenly. It was not that he was reluctant to leave Bethabara. Their original plans had been to go to Judea. He was hoping to see his old gambling friends. He had no money, but Abagtha would loan him enough to get into a game.

Once on the road, Simon began to talk excitedly about his prayer experience of the night before. "It was wonderful. I couldn't see God, but he was there all around me. I didn't hear an audible voice, but I knew what we were supposed to do today."

"Will you shut up!" Judas assented to the public prayers of the priests and had learned some prayers at the synagogue school he had attended as a child, but he was not inclined to make a personal petition to a deity that he couldn't see or hear.

Startled, Simon replied, "I'm sorry. I thought you would want to know why Jesus spends so much time in prayer. He has to."

"He also said to pray in secret," Judas retorted.

"I'm sorry. I thought you would be interested," Simon replied lamely.

"I'm not." Judas was surly. Their relationship was strained nearly to the breaking point as they continued toward Pella.

They reached Pella about noon and began to inquire about a place to stay. The first place where they stopped, they were given a flat "No!" At the second place, a buxom woman came to the gate in answer to their knock.

"I don't have room for you, and if you are John the Baptist's disciples, you won't want to stay. My advice to you is get out of town as fast as you can," she said gesturing down the street they had come up.

Judas and Simon looked in the direction of the gesture. An angry mob filled the street. There was no way to go back that way. They hurried off in the opposite direction, increasing their pace as the angry shouts grew louder and closer. Finally they broke into a flat out run for their lives as stones started sailing past. The mob stopped at the village limits and the two stopped to catch their breath in the shade of a eucalyptus tree.

"Guess we'll have to shake the dust off our feet against that town," Simon chuckled as he shook one foot.

"It sure looks like it." Judas laughed as he tried to shake both feet at once and fell down. They both rolled around on the ground in laughter. Then they sobered as they realized the symbolism of what they had done. They had just condemned the village to destruction, but the tension between them was broken. They were human, and humans sometimes find the ludicrous in the most solemn act.

Resuming their journey, they approached Jabesh-Gilead with fear, expecting no different reception than they had just received at Pella. However, they braced themselves and asked the gatekeeper about hospitality.

"Oh, yes, Adah will be happy for you to stay at her house. She is so lonely since Habiah died. He had no brothers and she has no sons. She loves to entertain strangers." The gatekeeper was very voluble and reluctant to let them go.

They had difficulty in finding the house although he had told them three times. Unfortunately, each time he had told them a different way. Finally, they asked a small boy playing in the street. He didn't say anything, just pointed to the house.

Adah was a friendly, outgoing person. It almost seemed that she had been expecting them. When they told her that they were disciples of Jesus of Nazareth, she was ecstatic.

"I heard about him when we were at the Temple last year. It was the last time that Habiah was able to go to the Temple. He went to the Temple every year while he was alive. He was such a good man. I am so glad you came. My sister, Ohea, is a disciple. She lives in Capernaum and she heard Jesus at the seaside."

Adah never stopped talking. A slave brought water to wash their feet. Only after they had been served a meal and shown to their quarters did Adah retire to her room. Simon went to the rooftop to pray and Judas went to sleep.

They were awakened early in the morning by a hubbub of voices in the courtyard. Adah had slipped out to tell a sick friend, "The disciples of Jesus of Nazareth are here, perhaps they can heal you."

She had sent her servants to tell others who were crippled, blind or hurt. And so it was the whole city had heard by daybreak.

The morning meal was already prepared, and the two disciples ate heartily. The crowd watched hungrily while they ate. It was not unusual for poor people to watch others eat. They were used to being hungry and considered themselves fortunate to have even one meal a day. They had come to be healed, not to eat.

As soon as they had finished eating, Judas and Simon began preaching and healing. They spent two whole days in Jabesh-Gilead, never leaving Adah's courtyard, for people continued to come.

From Jabesh-Gilead they went to Dion, where they were again well received. From Dion they went north to Capitolis and Gadera. They didn't encounter any more opposition; nevertheless, they were glad to get back to Galilee. They continued on to Capernaum where Jesus and the other disciples were waiting for them.

With excitement and eagerness they told of their experiences. "We saw sick people healed when we laid hands on them. Those who were crippled had their bones straightened, the deaf were able to hear and the blind could see. Even the devils were subject to us," Simon said exultantly.

"Yes, I gave you authority over the devils, but that is not nearly as important as having your names written in heaven," Jesus said.

Somehow, these were not the words that Judas had expected and hoped for. Instead of being grateful for a job well done, he expected them to be glad just to be in the Kingdom. Jesus didn't even have a throne, yet, although he probably would have soon. Except for that one town of Pella, they had good reception in Perea. The other five teams reported equally good results.

CHAPTER 12

MAKING A KING

Judas awakened from a very refreshing night's sleep. He had relaxed from the tension of the tour. Although he and Simon had reconciled their differences over prayer, he had not shared Simon's enthusiasm for the work. He had endured it, because he knew that he had to share in the campaign in order to share in the glory.

After he had eaten a cold breakfast left by the others, he noticed James and John talking to two men who were strangers to him, but evidently not to the other disciples, for they crowded around them as though they were old friends. They were dressed in distinctive Judean clothing and Judas wondered if they might have news from Kerioth (his hometown).

Drawing Simon aside, he asked, "Who are these men?"

"They are disciples of John the Baptist and they have come to tell Jesus that King Herod has had John beheaded."

"I knew that Herod had put him in prison. But I didn't think that he intended to kill him."

"It seems as though the king got drunk at his birthday party and asked his stepdaughter, Salome, to dance for his guests. He liked her dance so well that he offered her anything she wanted, up to half his kingdom. Her mother told her to ask for John the Baptist's head on a platter. I don't think the king wanted to kill John, but he didn't want to lose face in front of his guests."

Judas had heard the other disciples speak of John the Baptist, and he knew that at least James and John had been John's disciples before they became Jesus' disciples, but he himself had never seen him. Some of his friends from Kerioth had been baptized by John.

"What do you suppose they will do now?" he asked of Simon.

"I don't know. They buried John's body and came here to tell Jesus."

Matthew came toward them and said, "Come on, you two, we're going across the lake."

They all crowded into the boat with Jesus and set sail for the other side, leaving a crowd of people who had already started gathering on the Galileean shore. Crowds still made Judas nervous, and he was relieved to be leaving them behind.

"I think we are going to take a little vacation," he overheard John say to James.

"I could use a little rest," James replied. "That tour of Judea about wore me out."

So they, James and John, were the team that went to Judea. Envy and suspicion filled Judas' mind. It seemed to him that James and John always got the best jobs. Did Simon know where they had gone? He had seemed so positive that God had told him in answer to prayer where he and Judas were to go. James and John would have had to go through Bethabara on their way to Judea; do you suppose Simon had talked to them instead of going up to the housetop? Judas overheard more conversation.

"Do you remember that woman at Sychar?" James asked Andrew.

"Do you mean the one that left her waterpots at the well and went into town and brought the whole town back with her to see the Messiah?" Andrew recalled.

"We stayed at her house when we went down to Judea at her insistence. She married that man she was living with and you never saw a happier couple."

Judas felt ashamed that he had even imagined that Simon had secretly talked to James and John. It had not occurred to him that they had gone through Samaria. (To avoid going through Samaria, Jews crossed the Jordan at Bethabara and traveled down the eastern bank of Jordan).

As soon as James and John had told their experiences in Judea, Andrew and James, son of Alpheus, related their stories about their tour of Western Galilee. Jesus did not participate in the conversation, but sat in the back of the boat with a sad and weary look on his face. Judas guessed that it was because his friend, John the Baptist, was dead. He understood that John had started proclaiming the Kingdom of Heaven before Jesus did. He wondered what effect John's death might have on the Kingdom.

He had a premonition that things were going to be rougher for them. That one town chased them out because they thought that he and Simon were disciples of John the Baptist. Maybe that was why Jesus was crossing the Lake of Galilee. Ituraea, Trachonits, and associated districts in the northeast were King Philip's province, and they would be safe from Herod Antipis, who had ordered John the Baptist to be beheaded.

They landed on the eastern shore of the lake and prepared to relax for the day, but it was not to be. Barely had the boat been pulled on to the rocky shore until the distant sound of many voices reached them from the northern shore of the lake. The sound grew louder and they could distinguish human forms coming toward them.

"It's those people we left on the other side of the lake!" Peter exclaimed.

"How did they do that?" Judas asked.

"Oh, they went around the head of the lake. The Jordan River is pretty shallow at this time of the year. It's not too much farther by land. We had to row all the way against the wind. You can walk faster on land than you can row a boat in water."

Jesus arose from where he had been resting and went to meet the people. All day he healed and taught. As the sun was sinking low in the western sky, Jesus asked Philip, "Where are we going to buy bread for these people to eat?"

Judas was standing nearby, so Philip asked him how much money there was in the money bag.

"Two hundred denarii." Judas always knew what their balance was.

"Two hundred denarii won't buy enough food for everyone in this crowd to have even a morsel," Philip told Jesus as he walked back to him. "Lord, you're the only one who knows how we are going to feed all these people."

Andrew overheard the conversation. "Here is a boy with two fish and five loaves of bread, but what good is that in feeding all this mob?"

"Tell everyone to sit down in twelve rows of fifty with a space between each fifty and with eight groups of fifty in each row. Now, you Twelve get your fruit baskets out of the boat." (The twelve apostles each had a wicker basket that they used to gather fruit and other provisions given to them by supporters of the Kingdom).

Jesus then took the two fish and loaves and gave thanks to God. Afterward he said to Judas, "Hand me your basket, Judas."

Judas watched as he broke off a piece of bread and put it in his basket. Jesus then pinched off a piece of fish and added to it.

"Go down this first row and give to the people," Jesus said as he handed the basket back to Judas. He passed it to the first fifty. Everybody took huge handfuls. When they had all taken some, Judas took the basket expecting it to be empty. It was full! He handed it to the next fifty. The contents of the basket did not diminish until he came to the end of the row. The other apostles did the same. When they came back with their empty baskets, Jesus said, "Now, gather up the remnants. We don't want to waste any."

When they had picked up the scraps of fish and bread that the people had dropped, the baskets were again full.

It had been a full day. They had crossed the lake to escape the crowds and get a little rest, but the crowds had followed. Jesus seemed not to be able to resist an opportunity to heal and teach people. Judas supposed it was something that had to be done if Jesus were going to be king. He sensed that the people were ready to proclaim Jesus king.

"KING OF THE JEWS! KING OF THE J EWS!" The sound swelled as it passed from rank to rank. "JESUS OF NAZARETH, KING OF THE JEWS! JESUS OF NAZARETH, KING OF THE JEWS!"

Then they started an antiphony. One rank shouted, "HE IS KING!"

Another rank answered, "KING OF ISRAEL!"

Still another shouted, "JESUS OF NAZARETH!"

Others answered, "KING OF THE JEWS!"

Judas thrilled at the sound of it. Rank upon rank shouting in rhythm, like a majestic choir. The Twelve started to join in, but Jesus beckoned them back into the boat. He dismissed the crowd and slipped away into the mountains.

Judas and the rest of the Twelve were in the boat rowing back toward Capernaum. It didn't make sense. Why did Jesus want them to go back across the lake? The crowd was headed for Jerusalem to keep the Passover. What better time to proclaim Jesus king? People from all over Israel would be at Jerusalem to keep the Passover. Jesus could march at the head of the crowd, and they would be met at Jerusalem by an even larger crowd.

Instead, here they were in a boat headed back to Capernaum and Jesus was not even with them. He had gone off into the mountains to pray. Judas knew that. Didn't he ever get tired of praying? It seemed to Judas that it was time for action, not praying. Judas himself had no desire to pray. He had gone through the rituals to keep up appearances. After that outburst with Simon, he had stopped faking it. He had performed about as many miracles as Simon had on their tour, and Simon had lost all that sleep, praying. Yet, Jesus seemed to think that prayer was important and he knew that Jesus was doing just that. It was now night. The stars shown brightly. There was a head wind.

"Judas, would you take a turn at the oars?" Peter's voice broke into Judas' musings.

"Sure, if Simon will team with me," Judas replied.

"Of course, I'll take a turn," Simon said. "It looks like we are all going to have to take a turn. That wind is against us."

"We don't seem to be making any headway at all," Matthew said.

"We haven't made much," John said. "If that wind doesn't

stop, it will take all night to cross the lake." John had paired with Peter and they were both strong rowers.

"It should die down soon. It's the cold air coming off the mountains. We couldn't live in the Jordan Valley if it didn't cool off at night," James observed.

"Speaking of cold air, hand me my cloak," John said. "I got hot and sweaty while I was rowing, and now I'm chilly."

James' observation about the wind did not prove to be correct. Instead, the wind got stronger and it seemed that the boat was going backward. Judas and Simon, Bartholomew and Philip struggled and strained, but they couldn't gain against the wind.

"Look! Do you see what I see?" Simon screamed.

Judas did indeed see what Simon saw—a man walking toward them on the water. They had been facing the stern of the boat as they pulled at the oars. Judas felt a chill go up his spine, and the hairs on the back of his neck rise. It couldn't be human. A man couldn't walk on the water, and whatever it was, it was walking on the water. It came abreast of them and was walking right past the boat. By this time the four had dropped the oars and all of them were paralyzed with fear. Stark terror brought a simultaneous scream to their throats.

"Don't be afraid. It is I," Jesus' familiar voice called out.

"Lord, if it's really you, tell me to come to you," Peter said.

"Come on."

Peter threw a leg over the side of the boat and started walking toward Jesus as though he were on a sandy beach, but when he looked around and saw the waves, he started to sink.

"Save me, Lord," he shouted. Jesus reached out his hand and steadied Peter.

"Your faith is too small, Peter. Why did you doubt?"

What kind of man is this, Judas wondered? He walked on water as though it were a pebbled beach and that other time he had commanded the wind and waves and they obeyed him as men might obey a king. A king, well, of course, Jesus is a king! That is what they had been doing—preparing the nation for their king. A man who could command the wind could certainly command people.

"You really are the Son of God," the others cried. They were worshipping Jesus as though he were God himself. Judas was horrified. That was pure blasphemy. Jesus was an extraordinary man, but God? No, impossible!

CHAPTER 13

THE BEGINNING CANCER

They beached the boat, and eleven apostles went off to the mountains, but Judas slipped off to Capernaum. In the streets of Capernaum he met an old friend, Janus, a Roman who had helped him with his tax receipts when he was a publican.

"Hello, Judas, where have you been?" Janus said, hailing his friend. "I haven't seen you in more than a year. Hilen occupies your booth now."

"I am a disciple of Jesus of Nazareth," Judas replied reluctantly.

"You can't be serious? You'll never make any money following that crazy dreamer. I hear some of the Jews would like to make a king of him, but he wouldn't have it. Just as well, Rome doesn't want two kings in Galilee, and Herod would never give up his seat," Janus said, laughing.

Judas didn't reply. He hadn't really wanted to confess being Jesus' disciple, but he knew Janus was too astute to be deceived. How did he know what had happened yesterday on the other side of the lake? But that was his business. The Romans knew everything that was happening anywhere in the Empire.

"Come with me and I'll show you some fun," Janus said.

Judas hesitated. He didn't want to jeopardize his chances for a high place in the new government, if, indeed, Jesus was proclaimed king. Fraternizing with the Romans might be frowned on, although Jesus had healed the Roman centurion's slave.

"Don't worry, nobody will know, Lahad is a respectable Jew. He gives alms to all the beggars who come by." Janus seemed to know what Judas was thinking. He went with Janus, glad to talk to somebody besides those stuffy disciples.

Two beggars stretched out their hands as they approached Lahad's gate. Judas gave each of them a coin out of the Group's bag and dutifully recorded it. One man was horribly disfigured, the other a cripple, but it didn't occur to Judas to try to heal them. It was as though he were off duty.

Lahad gave them a hearty welcome, and after he learned that Judas was from Kerioth, his hometown, he inquired about mutual friends. Janus had disappeared, but Lahad didn't seem to notice. Presently they heard laughter and excited voices coming from another room. Lahad continued to speak of people he had known in Kerioth. Judas had difficulty keeping his mind on his host's conversation.

"Come in here, Ju," Janus said, beckoning from the open door through which he had disappeared.

Judas looked at Lahad. Lahad dismissed him with a smile and a wave of his hand. Evidently, he approved of what was going on in the other room.

Judas followed Janus into the next room. Four men were kneeling on a raised platform on the other side of the room. Judas had gambled in moderation when he had been a publican, but he hadn't the time, money or inclination since becoming a disciple. The disciples usually had enough to eat, but no personal cash. All the cash money that they received went into the common treasury, which Judas now carried in a bag.

There had been a few times they had picked heads of standing grain to eat. The Law did not prohibit picking standing heads of grain, provided it was eaten as it was picked. However, the Pharisees carped about them doing it on the Sabbath.

"Come on, Ju, get into the game. Let's see if you are as lucky as you used to be," Janus urged.

"Sure, Ju, you used to be pretty good at casting lots." The man addressing Judas looked up, and Judas recognized him. It was Jabniel, a publican from Jericho.

"I don't have any money," Judas explained.

"What's in the bag? I saw you give money to those beggars at the gate," Janus said.

"That money doesn't belong to me. I am treasurer for the Kingdom of Heaven," Judas further explained.

Janus laughed. "What kind of kingdom would want to give all its money to beggars?" he sneered. "Why don't you borrow enough to get into the game? With your luck you can probably double it in three or four throws."

What Janus was saying began to make sense to Judas. Often he had come home with what he brought, sometimes even more. Of course, he had sometimes returned with nothing, but that was part of the game. He only took with him as much money as he could afford to lose. If he lost it all, he quit. There was three hundred denarii in the bag. He decided to take one coin out of the bag. If he lost it, he could surely find a day's work to replace it.

"Call," the shooter said.

"One denarius on seven," Judas called. The other three matched it.

"Two denarii on four," the shooter said automatically, doubling the bets. It wasn't fair for the shooter to raise the bets after they were all in, and Judas was about to call him on it when the seven came up. They were all going to give Judas two denarii.

"Only what you bet. Only the shooter pays what he bet."

The shooter paid and left the game and it was Judas' turn to shoot. Judas never bet more than one denarius. If they raised, he dropped his turn. He lost a few times, but he won more.

"See, I told you that you were lucky," Janus said. They kept playing and one by one the other players dropped out.

"Looks like you and I are the only lucky ones tonight," Janus grinned. He began to win more throws than Judas. Finally, Judas had only one denarius left. He put it in his bag and stood.

"Wait a minute. What are you doing?" Janus asked.

"I'm going to quit with what I started with. My luck has changed and one more throw and I would be in the hole."

"Oh, come on, Ju, be a sport. Your luck can change in one throw."

"You already have all that was in the pot. Why would you want one more denarius?"

"Tell you what I'll do. There is more in this pile than what you've got in the bag. Just to show you what a good sport I am, I'll put it all on the next throw against what you have in the bag."

Judas couldn't resist. Here was a chance to more than double the money. There was a good five hundred denarii in front of Janus.

"All right," Judas assented weakly.

"You call." One call was all that was needed since the winner would take all.

"Seven." It had been his lucky number all evening and the odds favored it. Janus picked up the dice, blew on them and threw them against the padded wall. One bounced back into the light, one spot on the top side. The other rolled into a dark corner. Jabniel, who had dropped out of the game but remained to watch, went to find a candle. Judas, who didn't pray, found himself praying silently, "Oh, God, let it be a six." Jabniel came back with a lighted candle.

"What do you know. It's another one," Jabniel chortled.

"I win!" Janus exulted.

Judas was stunned. Mechanically, he emptied the bag on the pile of coins in front of Janus and went out into the night.

The fourth watch was beginning when he reached the house of Mary of Magdala. Jesus and the rest of the disciples were asleep in the courtyard. He wrapped his cloak around himself and lay down to a sleepless night. The empty bag tied securely under his cloak matched the emptiness of his heart.

There was no feasible way to replace the stolen money; he had to admit to himself that it was stolen. He had deluded himself into believing that the one small piece that he had used to get into the game was just borrowed. If he had lost it, he might have found a day's work and replaced it, although he didn't know when he would have found time to work as a day laborer, even for one day. He didn't have anything that he could sell, at least not for three hundred denarii. That was a whole year's wages! Maybe someone would give the Group a large gift. Finally, just before daybreak, he came to a satisfactory decision. He didn't have to give an accounting until after the Passover. Until then, he would just brazen it out. It was not the first time he had brazened his way through similar situations when he had been a publican. In the meantime, something might happen to enable him to replace the missing money.

CHAPTER 14

CANNIBALISM

"Wake up, Judas, it's the third hour. This is the Sabbath day and we are going to the synagogue." Matthew gently shook his friend awake.

Judas wished Matthew would just go away, but fearing to arouse suspicions of his whereabouts the previous night and the late hour of his return, he shook himself awake and said, "I must have overslept."

"You sure have," Matthew chuckled. "Mary has carried a fresh pot of water from the well. Splash some of it on your face. It will help you wake up."

Judas flashed a smile at Matthew and went to the water pot and washed his face. It did help to clear the sleep from his eyes, but he had a tension headache. He didn't say anything about it, and Matthew didn't seem to suspect anything.

Hurrying to the synagogue, they slipped quietly through the right side door. The synagogue was crowded, so no one noticed their entrance.

"O bestow on your people, Israel, great peace forever. For you art king, and Lord of all peace. And it is good in your eyes to bless your people, Israel, at all times and at every hour with your peace!" With these words a priest was standing with his hands raised toward the people pronouncing the last blessing from the Talmud; turning toward the sanctuary he offered a free prayer in his own words.

When the priest had finished the prayer, Judas stole a quick glance at the congregation and recognized some of the same people to whom he had served food the day before.

His attention was refocused when the minister brought out a
roll of the law, and very carefully took it out of the case and handed
it to the first of seven readers, who would each read three verses.
The first reader was a descendant of Aaron. He was followed by a
Levite and then five ordinary Israelites. An interpreter stood at the
side of each reader and translated the Hebrew into Aramic. After
the Law had been read, a section from the prophet Daniel was
read and a methmurgeman interpreted it: "In the time of these
kings, the God of heaven will set up a kingdom that will never be
destroyed, nor will it be left to another people. It will crush all
those kingdoms and bring them to an end, but it will, itself, endure
forever. This is the meaning of the vision of the rock cut out of the
mountain, but not by human hands—a rock that broke the iron,
the bronze, the clay, the silver and the gold to pieces."

Jairus, president of the synagogue, rose and said, "Jesus of
Nazareth will proclaim the sermon today."

Jesus stepped up and sat down in the lecture chair.

"Teacher! How did you get here?" A man in the congregation
spoke loudly.

Jesus replied, "The truth is that all you want is the food I gave
you yesterday. You weren't interested in the miracles. You shouldn't
be concerned about perishable things like food. You need to spend
your energy looking for eternal life that I, the Son of Man, can give
you. For the Father has sent me for this very purpose."

The man who had spoken before was apparently the spokesman
for the others, for he spoke again. "What must we do, in order to
do the works of God."

Jesus answered, "This is the work of God, that you believe in
him whom he has sent."

"What sign do you do, that we may see and believe that you
are the Messiah. Why not give us bread every day as Moses gave
our fathers in the wilderness?"

"My father gave your fathers bread in the wilderness, not Moses.
And now my Father wants to give you the real bread from heaven.
The real bread is a person. He has been sent by God from heaven
to give his life for the world."

"Give us this bread all the time."

Jesus said to them, "I am that bread. No one coming to me will ever be hungry again; those believing in me will never thirst. But the problem is, as I have told you before, you haven't believed even though you have seen me. But there are some who will come to me, the ones that my Father has given me, and I will never turn them away."

"I didn't come from heaven to do my will. I came to do the will of him that sent me. And his will is that I should lose none of those that he gives me, but raise them up at the last day. His will is that everyone who sees the Son and believes in him should have everlasting life."

The Jews began murmuring among themselves, "What is he talking about? 'Coming down from heaven?' Is he trying to tell us that he came down from heaven?"

Jesus answered, "Don't murmur among yourselves. No one can come to me unless the Father draws him. It is written in the prophets, 'They shall be taught by God.' Those who are taught by God will be drawn to me. The only one who has actually seen the Father is the one who came down from heaven. With all earnestness, I tell you that anyone who believes in me already has eternal life! I am the bread of life. There was only physical life in the bread your fathers ate in the wilderness. I am the eternal living bread that came down from heaven: If anyone eats this bread, he shall live forever; and I shall give this, which is my flesh, for the life of the world. Unless you eat my flesh and drink my blood, you cannot have eternal life in you."

The Jews started murmuring among themselves again. "How can this man give us his flesh to eat?"

Jesus replied, "My flesh is the real bread, and my blood is the real drink. If you eat my flesh and drink my blood, I will become part of you and you will become part of me."

Judas had been listening very intently. What was Jesus talking about? The thought of eating human flesh and drinking blood was nauseating. Why that was cannibalism! No wonder the Jews didn't believe in him. They didn't even drink animal blood, much less human blood. The longer he listened, the more repulsed he was by what Jesus was saying. He burst out, "Who can listen to this?"

Even some of the rest of the Twelve admitted that it was hard to understand.

Jesus turned to them and said, "Is this offensive to you? What will you think when you see the Son of Man going back to heaven? It is the Spirit that gives eternal life. The flesh is only temporary. But there are some of you who do not believe me."

Judas thought to himself, "Of course, there are some who do not believe. Who could believe this nonsense about eating his flesh and drinking his blood?"

Jesus said, "You can't come to me unless the Father attracts you to me."

When he said that, almost everyone left the synagogue. Jesus turned to the Twelve and asked, "Are you going, too?"

Simon Peter spoke up. "Teacher, to whom would we go? You are the only one that can give words of eternal life, and we believe and know that you are the holy Son of God."

Then Jesus said, "I have chosen you Twelve and one of you is a devil." Judas' heart began to pound. What did Jesus mean? But he didn't dare ask him.

CHAPTER 15

GENTILE COUNTRY

Arla was becoming more and more worried about her daughter, Tara. Tara had been a happy obedient child until she was ten years old. She had taken her to a witch doctor to have an ulcer on her arm healed. There had been some disagreement over his fee, and Arla walked out without paying him anything.

The arm had healed, but Tara began to be disobedient. Arla had asked her to go to the village well after water. The water pot was not a large one, and Tara had managed it many times before.

"Go get it yourself; I wasn't born to be your slave!" Tara yelled defiantly.

Arla tried to spank her.

"Don't you dare lay a hand on me. You g—d—f—old whore," she screamed at her mother. Then she grabbed the water pot and threw it against the wall, breaking it into pieces. She looked at her mother with hate-filled eyes, and Arla was frightened of her own daughter. She would just have to wait until Ahnsted came in from the fields.

Tara had rushed from the house after the broken pot incident and spent the rest of the day under a carob tree. Occasionally, she screamed the hopeless, hair-raising scream of the damned; mostly she babbled an incoherent half-laughing, half-mocking jabber.

When Ahnsted came home, Arla told him how Tara had acted.

"When I get through with her, she'll not break any more pots," he said determinedly.

"Don't you come near me, you g—d—s—of a b—." She was like a little tornado as she rushed into her father, biting and screaming and scratching. Ahnsted was paralyzed by the unexpected onslaught. He literally ran back into the house, his clothing in shreds. He had bites and scratches all over him. It was as though he had encountered a leopard instead of his own daughter.

Tara returned to the house sometime during the night. She didn't attack her parents anymore. She didn't eat or sleep. She was sullen and morose. Occasionally, she would scream and be seized by a convulsion. Afterward, she would lie on the floor a long time, seemingly lifeless. Most of the time she stared into space with fear-filled eyes. Her physical condition deteriorated rapidly. As she got weaker, she allowed Arla near and almost became docile.

Two days later she actually spoke to her mother. "Mamma. They're coming after me tomorrow. Oh, mamma, I'm so scared!"

"Who's coming after you, dear?" Arla asked.

But Tara never replied; she was again babbling incoherently.

At the third hour that same morning, there was a knock at the gate; it was her friend, Helga. Helga lived in a small village just across the border in Galilee. Arla was not a Jew, but she regarded the Jewess Helga as her best friend. They shared their inmost secrets.

As they embraced, Helga asked, "How is Tara?" Having no children of her own, she had become very fond of Tara. Arla burst into tears. Helga wrapped her arms around Arla again. Great sobs shook her body. Finally she was able to sob out the whole hurting story.

"Don't worry," Helga said. "Bring her over to my house. Jesus of Nazareth and his disciples are staying there."

"Who is Jesus of Nazareth?"

"He is a great healer. He has healed all kinds of diseases, and some say that he can even raise the dead."

"Do you think he could help Tara?"

"I know he can. He has thrown out devils many times."

"I'll see if I can get her to go."

Unlike her prior reactions, Tara offered no resistance to Arla's touch, but allowed her to lead her to Helga's village. She seemed unaware of her surroundings, but continued to stare into space with a fear-filled face.

They found Jesus and his disciples outside the village. There

were no crowds of sick and crippled people as there had been at
Capernaum. Jesus was teaching the disciples when Helga, Arla
and Tara arrived. They listened quietly for a while, but Arla could
restrain herself no longer. "O, Lord, Son of David, help me. My
daughter is possessed of a devil, and it torments her all the time."

Jesus didn't seem to hear her, but continued with his teaching.
However, his disciples heard and were annoyed, saying, "Send her
away. We don't need her kind around begging." Her clothing and
facial features clearly identified her as being a Syro-Phoenician.

Arla's heart sank. Her last hope was gone. Tomorrow her
daughter would be in hell. The implication of Tara's last intelligible
words, "They are coming after me tomorrow," became clear to
Arla. She knew that her daughter's last hours were a certain, fearful
waiting for death and then everlasting torment.

But Jesus was speaking to her. "I am not sent to Gentiles, only
to Jews."

Arla fell on her knees before Jesus. "Lord, help me!" she cried.

Jesus said, "It isn't right to throw the children's bread to the
dogs."

Arla knew what Jesus meant. She had heard the epithet "Gentile
dog" often in this little border village where she had lived all her
life. Well, she would be a dog if that was needed to get help. "That
is true, Lord, but the little puppies may eat the scraps that are left
after the children finish eating."

"Lady, you have much faith. Your request is granted; your
daughter is healed."

Arla lifted her head. Jesus was smiling. She stood and turned
toward Tara. Tara was smiling. The vacant stare was gone. She rushed
to her mother's arms. "Oh, mamma, I feel so good inside," she cried.
The nightmare of the last few days was just that: a nightmare that was
gone with the coming of the Son of Righteousness.

- -

Judas was tired and bored. They had spent two months from
April to June near the border of Phoenicia. It was pretty country,

but except for that one incident with that Gentile woman and her demon-possessed daughter, there had been little activity. It was a stupid way to start a kingdom if, indeed, there was going to be a kingdom. Jesus spent much time teaching them about the kingdom of Heaven, as he called it. Judas' mind got bogged down with all those spiritual details. He couldn't understand why Jesus didn't take over the government like the Maccabees had done. He could do some of his miracles to avoid bloodshed. Personally, he would like to see some of those fat Sadducees and cold Pharisees bleed a little.

Of course, there were the Romans. They didn't really care who was king of Israel as long as taxes were paid and order was kept.

Judas' musings came back to yesterday. What would it be like to be possessed of the devil? That girl had a funny look in her eyes. He wondered if he could exorcise devils. Simon had when they were on their Decapolis campaign, but he had never tried it. He would try it when and if he got an opportunity.

CHAPTER 16

SIN, UNCONFESSED

After spending three more days in Phoenicia, they were on the road again. They left Gentile territory and went south to the Decapolis region. There Jesus resumed his healing ministry. A deaf and dumb man was healed and many others with infirmities. The crowds began coming again, and Jesus fed four thousand in a miracle similar to the five thousand at the lakeside.

Judas was encouraged. Maybe Jesus could still get enough people together to march on Jerusalem and take over the throne. They crossed the Sea of Galilee and landed at Magdala. As soon as the people of Galilee learned that Jesus was back in their territory, they began coming to him in crowds. The Pharisees and Sadducees mingled with the crowds and challenged Jesus, "Show us a sign from heaven."

Jesus said, "When the sky is red at sunset, you say that tomorrow will be fair. If the sky is red at sunrise, you know that it is going to rain. If you can tell the signs of the sky, why can't you tell the signs of the times? This adulterous generation keeps looking for a sign. The only sign you will get is that of the prophet, Jonah. As Jonah was inside the whale three days and three nights, so will the Son of Man be inside the earth three days and three nights."

Judas didn't have any idea what Jesus meant. He had no love for the Pharisees and Sadducees, but he couldn't understand why Jesus couldn't accommodate them a little bit. After all, they had a lot of political power. He liked to see signs himself. However, Jesus was probably right—if you yielded to their whims, they would want the best jobs in the new kingdom, and he wanted them.

Once again, they set sail across Lake Galilee.

"I'm hungry." James (called the less to distinguish him from James the brother of John) was speaking. "Would you hand me a piece of bread out of the basket, Judas?"

"I forgot to buy any," Judas lied. The empty bag under his cloak was filled with deceit and distress. As treasurer, he was expected to buy food for the Twelve, as well as give to the poor.

"Watch out for the yeast of the Pharisees," Jesus said. Judas was relieved. The only bakery in Capernaum was owned by a Pharisee.

"It is a good thing that I forgot to buy bread. I would have had to buy it from a Pharisee," Judas defended himself.

"Oh, you of little faith! Don't you remember the five loaves that fed five thousand people?" Jesus remonstrated. "How many did you have left?"

"Twelve," James, the less, answered.

"How many basketfuls had you left when four thousand were fed?"

"Seven," James said.

"Can't you understand that I wasn't meaning literal bread?" The teaching of the Pharisees had been Jesus' warning, but it had diverted attention away from Judas' supposed oversight. Never again did they lack for anything to eat. Everywhere they went, people insisted they rest awhile and eat and drink with them. Occasionally, someone would give Judas some coins to put in the money bag. Just having money in the bag again lifted Judas' spirit. It was still far short of the gambling loss, but not empty.

The crossing of Lake Galilee was without incident and landing near Bethsaida Julias, they walked on into the city, but continued on through the city in a northerly direction.

"Where are we going?" asked Thomas of James, John's brother.

"I don't know," James said. "Do you want me to ask John? He usually knows where Jesus is going."

"Don't bother. I was just noticing how pretty the view is from up here." Thomas gestured back to the way they had come. They had traveled twenty-five miles and climbed six hundred eighty nine feet. The entire Jordan valley was spread out behind them.

While the rest set up camp by the Waters of Merom, Peter and John fished in the little basin formed by the Jordan River in its headlong rush to Lake Galilee. The sun was sinking behind the mountains in the west, but sunlight still flickered and danced on the snow-covered peak of Mount Hermon, which dominated the darkening sky in the North.

Thomas, the practical one, had built a fire in anticipation of the fish that Peter and John would catch. His anticipation was soon rewarded with a dozen mountain trout, which they had caught with hook and line. After cleaning the fish, Thomas laid them on the hot coals. The fish were soon done and they ate their fill. It had been a long day, and they had finally gotten away from the crowds and the hectic pace of the last few weeks.

"I'll put some more wood on the fire," Thomas said. "It's getting chilly since the sun went down."

"Good idea," said James, as he found a spot closer to the fire and lay down, wrapping his cloak about him.

Judas remained where he was, a little apart from the rest. No one noticed since he had selected the spot before Thomas built the fire. There was very little conversation. Even Peter, who was usually voluble, had little to say. Weariness soon brought slumber to the Group.

"Come and dine, children!" Jesus' voice rang out in the crisp morning air.

Judas opened his eyes to see the sun barely peeping over the Eastern mountains. When he had closed his eyes last night, Jesus had gone to a nearby mountain to pray. Now he had fish cooked and bread baked on the hot coals of fire. Judas was tempted to ask Jesus where the bread and fish had come from since they had eaten all the fish and bread last night and there was no more grain from which to grind meal. Maybe Jesus had performed another miracle.

"I needed two assarion to buy bread." Jesus answered Judas' question before it was asked. Judas put his hand involuntarily on the empty money bag. As they were leaving Capernaum two days before, a man had thrust two assarion into Judas' hand and hurried away. While Judas slept, Jesus had taken it and gone into Kadesh, the ancient city of refuge of Naphtali, to buy bread. The fishing line that Peter had used last evening was wet, an indication that it had been used that morning. Jesus had bought bread, caught fish and rebuilt the fire, all before the dawn, while they slept. Jesus knew about the empty bag. Judas braced himself for the confrontation, but Jesus sat waiting for him to confess. It was the accepted time to say, "Lord, you know the bag is empty. I lost it all in a dice game." Judas knew that Jesus would forgive him, but he couldn't humble himself before the other disciples, so he said nothing. Jesus did not force him to confess.

"This is the best fish that I have ever tasted," said John.

Jesus smiled. "The mountain air has sharpened your appetite, John."

"This is the first time we have eaten trout. The water in Lake Galilee is too warm for them to live," Peter said. "I can't tell the difference, but some people think that trout is the best tasting fish." They bantered around the campfire for an hour until the sun was high enough to make the campsite uncomfortably warm.

They continued on up the Jordan Valley all that day toward Caesarea Philippi. Most of the time they followed the Roman Road, which made walking much easier. Occasionally, they met a caravan going down to Capernaum. The little donkeys were like warehouses on legs, almost hidden beneath the pots and clothing and rugs and various other articles that the merchants hoped to sell in Capernaum.

As the Twelve continued their upward trek, they passed through a narrow, rich valley. Vines and mulberry trees made a corridor and even arched over the road in many places. As they came out of the valley, they ascended through a rocky wilderness of hills.

"Let's rest awhile," Simon suggested to Judas. The two of them stopped and sat down. Everyone else agreed with Simon and Judas by sitting down, too.

"Look! Judas, you can see Lake Merom," Simon continued. "It looks so far away. I can't believe we have come so far."

"We have only come twelve miles, but we are looking down on it. It makes it seem much farther. Ten minutes ago, you couldn't have seen it at all," Bartholomew said. "I used to come up here when I worked for Zaanan. I led his caravan of donkeys through these mountains."

"I didn't know that," Peter said.

"I just worked for him one summer. He learned that he could sell his goatskins to the traders going through Capernaum. Of course, he didn't get as much money for them, but he didn't have to keep a string of burros around all year."

"That left you without a job, didn't it?" Judas asked.

"Not really. Zaanan gave me enough sheep to start a flock of my own," Bartholomew answered. "But I do miss these mountains. See, up there ahead of us is Mount Hermon with his snowy locks. Over there is the Eastern Mountains." He gestured with his right hand. "And over here is the Western Mountains," he said, gesturing with his left hand.

"Who shall ascend into the hill of the Lord? Or who shall stand in his holy place?" Andrew started the ancient psalm.

Philip answered with the antiphony, "He that has clean hands and a pure heart."

Soon they were all singing as loud as they could, "Lift up your heads, O you gates and be you lifted up, you everlasting doors; and the King of Glory shall come in." It was truly a time of worship there in that outdoor cathedral.

When they had finished the psalm, Jesus arose to resume their upward trek. The road ascended for a short time, then descended to a plain where all the springs of Jordan unite. As they passed an unharvested ripe wheat field, they broke off a few handfuls of grain and rubbed it out to assuage a hunger that had grown since they had eaten the fish early that morning.

After walking another half hour, they came to and crossed a bridge over Jordan where basalt walls made a narrow channel causing the water to be swift and deep. As they continued their trek, they passed by the ancient city of Dan.

Jesus called the Twelve together to teach them. They had difficulty in finding a place to sit. The whole area was solid rock with a few loose stones on top. After they had selected stones at random to sit on, Jesus began, "Whom do people say that I am?"

"King Herod thinks that you are John the Baptist risen from the dead," John said.

"Some of the people believe that you are the Prophet Elijah, who is supposed to come before the Messiah," James said.

"I have heard people say that you are Jeremiah, or one of the other prophets," Philip said.

"Whom do you believe that I am?" Jesus asked.

"You are the Christ, the son of the Living God," Peter said calmly and confidently.

"You are blessed, Simon. You didn't learn that from any human being, but it came directly from my Father in Heaven. You are Peter, a stone, and upon this solid rock, I will build my church and the gates of hell shall not prevail against it. I will give you the keys to the Kingdom. For some you will unlock the gates, and for others you will lock them."

Judas hadn't the slightest idea what Jesus was talking about, but he did understand that Peter believed that Jesus was God, and instead of rebuking Peter for blasphemy, Jesus had encouraged the stupid clod. One could expect something stupid to come out of Peter's mouth. His jaw was always working, but his brain (if he had one) didn't have any control over it. But for Jesus to accept such a ridiculous claim, and to say that God had revealed it to Peter was going too far; that was pure and bold blasphemy. If the chief priests knew about it, they would condemn Jesus to death. Maybe it was his duty to inform them. They might even pay for the information.

As if reading Judas' mind, Jesus was speaking, "We will be going back to Jerusalem in a few days. I will be arrested by the chief priests. They will condemn me to death, and I will be executed by the Romans. Three days later I will arise from the grave."

Peter jumped from his seat and took Jesus by the arm. "God forbid! This can't be!" he cried.

Jesus shook free of Peter and turned his back. "Get behind me, Satan. You are thinking from the human viewpoint, not God's way at all!"

Peter sat back down and Jesus continued to teach them. "If anyone still wants to follow me, he will have to give up his own desires and ideas. Whoever clutches his life will lose it. But, whoever lets go of his life, for my sake, will find it again. What have you gained if you have everything in the world and lose your life? What are you going to give in exchange for your life? For I, the Son of Man, shall come with my angels in the glory of my Father and judge each person according to his deeds. And some of you, who are standing here right now, will see me in my coming kingdom." With these words, Jesus finished speaking.

Judas' confusion deepened. He had just about given up on the kingdom idea since Jesus had refused to let the people make him king. Now, they had come up here to Caesarea Philippi to escape the Jews, which made good sense. Judas knew what Jesus said about being arrested and sentenced to death was a very real possibility if they went back to Jerusalem, even if Peter didn't want to believe it. He was beginning to understand now. God would send angels to protect them, just like he did for Elisha. Maybe there would be a kingdom after all.

CHAPTER 17

EPHER

Beriah was spent, both emotionally and physically. He had dragged little Epher out of the fire again. It would have been much worse if Kelita, Epher's older sister, hadn't pushed him away before he fell into the middle of the fire. Only one foot was burned as he thrashed about in the fit the devil had thrown him into.

Beriah was at his wit's end. Kelita couldn't watch Epher all the time; she needed to help her mother. Beriah himself would have been out working in his field if he hadn't been mending the harness for the oxen.

"Shalom, Beriah." The voice of Helon, his good friend from Caeserea Philippi startled him.

Beriah grabbed Helon and kissed him on both cheeks. "It is so good to see you, Helon. Is your wife well?" Beriah continued to ask about the health of all Helon's family members and was assured they were all well. It was then Helon's turn to ask about Beriah's family.

"They are all well except little Epher. He has a devil, and it throws him to the ground and he thrashes about and froths at the mouth. At times it throws him into the fire and he is burned. This morning, Kelita pushed him away from the fire before he fell in." Beriah didn't expect his friend to be able to help, but sometimes telling a sympathetic friend eases the worry.

"Beriah, I may have some good news for you. I think the great healer from Galilee, Jesus of Nazareth, is in this area. From what I have heard about him, he can throw the devil out of your son."

"I have never heard of him. Why should he be in this area if he is a Galileean?"

"You have never heard of Jesus of Nazareth? Travelers from Jerusalem pass through Caeserea Philippi almost every day, and they tell about the healer. Some say that he will be the next king of Israel."

"I don't go to Caeserea Philippi. Too many Gentiles for me."

"You will never get rich if you don't trade with the Gentiles. They are the ones who have the money to spend. They buy the expensive garments I get from Damascus and the spices and exotic jewels I get from Tyre and Sidon."

"My fields provide the food, and my herds provide the clothing for my family; what else could I want?"

"Right now you want the devil out of your son. Why don't we see if we can find Jesus of "Nazareth?"

"I'll do anything to get rid of that devil in little Epher. If you think this Jesus of Nazareth can do anything, we will start at once."

They went to Caeserea Philippi and began to inquire. Someone had seen Jesus and his disciples near the upper springs of Jordan. However, there was no one there when they arrived. As they were returning to the city they met a man, Cosan, whom Helon knew. Helon introduced Beriah and told of their search for Jesus and his disciples.

"You might try the synagogue. His custom is to go to the synagogue every Sabbath," Cosan said.

"How do you know that?" Helon asked.

"When I was in Capernaum I became a disciple, but I didn't know that he had come up here," Cosan replied.

They went to the synagogue. The ruler, Ibhar, remembered Jesus and the disciples being there, but where they had gone he didn't know.

"Why are you looking for him?" Ibhar asked.

"My son is possessed by a devil, and I have heard that Jesus of Nazareth can throw out devils," Beriah replied.

"He does it by the power of Beelzebub!" Ibhar shouted at Beriah.

They turned and hurried away from the agitated priest, but a man ran after them. "My name is Addi. I overheard what Ibhar said, and I know which way the Nazarene went, but we will have to hurry. They are a day's journey ahead of us. They stayed at my home last night and left at dawn. You, too, may stay at my home tonight."

"But you just said that we needed to hurry and we do want to hurry," Beriah said.

"My home is in the direction that you are going. We will reach it about dusk, and you sure don't want to go any farther into those mountains after dark," Addi said. They followed him to his home in the mountains. He lived a short distance from the trail that Jesus and his disciples had taken.

News of their arrival in Caeserea Philippi, and their purpose in looking for Jesus had spread around in that mysterious way that people had before modern communications. Curiosity on the part of the residents and malice on the part of the priests brought a party of twenty-five together by nightfall, ready to start from Caeserea Philippi the next morning to follow Beriah and Helon.

The next morning, Addi led the way north toward Mount Hermon. Ever upward they toiled all day. The thinner air and the climb was exhausting, but Addi urged haste with the admonition that they were already a day's journey behind. Some of Addi's friends did go back to Caeserea Philippi, but Beriah, spurred on by hope, never faltered. Epher rode along on a little donkey. He seemed docile enough now, but Beriah was in constant fear that the devil might seize him and cause him to fall off into one of the steep canyons that they were now passing.

Ibhar had seen Addi join Beriah and sought out the scribes and a visiting rabbi named Harum. Addressing them, he said, "Addi has conspired against us and is a guide to Beriah. Beriah is hoping the Nazarene can throw the devil out of his son."

"Didn't you tell him that Jesus throws out devils by the power of Beelzebub?" Harum asked.

"I did, but Helon is a disciple of the Nazarene and has convinced Beriah that he is a prophet," Ibhar said.

"We need go to catch them and stop this stupidity before it grows like it did in Galilee," Harum said. And so, a second party went to find Jesus and his disciples.

CHAPTER 18

THE COLD MOUNTAIN

It was cold. Judas shivered in his cloak. The rest of the disciples had gathered all the wood they could find and had built a fire. Peter, James and John had gone with Jesus higher up the mountain. Judas was seething on the inside. For this he had left a lucrative tax-collecting business, a cold God-forsaken mountain in the middle of the night. A cold wind came off the snow on the mountain. Even though it was night, the moonlight glistened on the snow, and it was light enough to see clearly.

He threw another piece of wood on the fire. He couldn't understand how the others could sleep as cold as it was. When they got down off this mountain, he was going to find some way to repay the stolen money (might have to sell himself as a slave . . . nothing could be worse than his present misery), and then he was quitting, kingdom or no kingdom.

He didn't know that he had gone to sleep, but the sun was shining and someone had built a new fire. He was actually warm. Thomas, the practical one, had found a hollow place in a rock and using another round stone for crude millstones had ground enough meal for corn cakes, which he was now baking on the coals of last night's fire.

"The Lord bless you, Thomas," said Bartholomew. "None of the rest of us thought to bring anything to eat."

"I think it's about ready to eat," Thomas said. He glowed from Bartholomew's praise but modestly ignored it.

"Jesus, Peter, James and John are still up on the mountain, praying. Matthew, will you bless the cakes?"

Matthew recited the ancient Hebrew blessing and passed the cakes to the other eight disciples and to himself.

They had just finished eating when they heard voices and a clatter of donkey feet on the stony path from whence they had come the day before.

"Someone is coming," Philip said.

"I didn't think anyone knew that we were up here," Matthew added.

"Maybe they are not looking for us," observed Nathaniel.

Beriah's party came into view and Beriah hailed them. After he had introduced himself, he explained his purpose and brought Epher before them. "My son, Epher, has a devil, and I was told at Caesarea Philippi that Jesus of Nazareth could throw out devils."

"He is not here now. He and three of our number have gone up the mountain to pray and have not returned," Matthew explained.

Just then Epher had a seizure and fell into the fire that they had baked the cakes on.

"Oh, my poor son," Beriah moaned as he pulled Epher from the fire. Fortunately, he was not hurt. His heavy clothing, the dying fire and his father's quick action prevented serious burns.

"We don't have to wait until Jesus comes down from the mountain," Judas said. "He gave us power to throw out devils." He, who had shrunk from healing when he and Simon had been on tour, reached out and placed his hand on Epher's shoulder. "In the name of Jesus of Nazareth, I command you to come out of him, you evil spirit."

"Take your hands off me!" Epher screamed and reached out and clawed at Judas' face. Judas retreated a few steps and the boy fell to the ground, thrashing about and foaming at the mouth, finally lying very still. After a few minutes of deathlike stillness, Epher began to move. Beriah helped his son to his feet. It was obvious that the demon had not been thrown out.

"It is apparent that you may as well go back home," taunted Ibhar, who had arrived during the confusion with the second party from Caesarea Philippi.

"He does it by the power of Beelzebub, anyway," Harum goaded.

"Maybe Beelzebub doesn't have any power in the mountains," a tagalong ruffian in the party said with a laugh.

Beriah lifted Epher onto the donkey's back and prepared to go back down the mountain. A look of extreme sad weariness came on his face, and every part of his body frame echoed the utter hopelessness he felt. His last hope was gone. Jesus of Nazareth couldn't help him. No one could.

The sound of footsteps sloshing through the melting snow brought all eyes toward the three coming down from the mountain. The eight remaining disciples (all but Judas) ran to meet Jesus, and all began to talk at once.

"What is all this confusion about?" asked Jesus as he came to the group deriding Beriah.

Beriah came and knelt at Jesus' feet. "My son is possessed of a demon, and I brought him to your disciples and they couldn't throw the demon out."

Jesus looked at the Twelve and said wearily, "How long will it be before you have any faith?" Turning to Beriah, he said, "Bring him here."

As Beriah helped Epher from his donkey, he had another seizure.

"How long has he been this way?" Jesus asked.

"Since he was a little boy, Lord. If you can help us, please do."

"Why do you say, 'If I can help'? All things are possible for those who believe."

"Lord, I believe. Help my unbelief!" Beriah cried out in uncertainty and desperation.

"You deaf and dumb spirit, come out of him and don't go into him again!"

Epher went into another convulsion that drained his strength and left him lifeless until some thought he was dead. After an interval of minutes, he began to move and soon stood upon his feet. His eyes were no longer dull and glassy, but bright with awareness.

"Abba, I feel good," the boy said.

After Beriah and his party had gone back down the mountain, Matthew asked, "Why couldn't we throw the demon out of Epher?"

With patience and tenderness Jesus said, "You just don't have faith. It takes prayer to throw this kind out."

Who cares whether we throw out demons, Judas thought. It was cold enough last night sitting by the fire without going up in the mountain to pray in the snowdrifts.

CHAPTER 19

DISSENSION

As soon as Beriah and his party had gone back down the mountain, Jesus and the Twelve broke camp and followed. As they descended to a warmer altitude, Judas' spirit revived and he even engaged Peter in conversation.

"It sure is good to get off that cold mountain," he said.

"I would have liked to have stayed up there forever," Peter replied enthusiastically.

"Are you beside yourself?" Judas snorted. "There is nothing up there but rocks and snow!"

"If you had gone to pray, you would have liked it better."

"Hey, what is this?" Judas retorted. "I wasn't asked to go."

"Neither was I, but John, James and I wanted to go with Jesus. The rest of you wanted to sleep."

"I suppose you think that you are going to be the greatest in the Kingdom!"

"You're the one who tried to throw the demon out of the boy and failed!" Peter hadn't seen it, but Matthew had told him what had happened.

"You're just a shoe latch looser!"

They were suddenly aware that the others were watching the disruptive scene they were creating. Peter hurried to catch up to James and John, and Judas fell in step with Matthew.

They reached Capernaum at the time to pay the temple tax. Those who collected tax for the temple accosted Peter on the street. "Doesn't your rabbi pay taxes?"

"Of course," Peter answered somewhat apologetically, since Capernaum was his hometown and he had always paid the temple tax promptly before. "I'll go get it." He went to find Judas, intending to pay the tax out of the Group's treasury.

Before he found Judas, he met Jesus, who said, "What do you think, Peter? Do kings collect taxes from their own sons or from the citizens of their kingdom?"

"From their citizens."

"Then the sons shouldn't have to pay taxes. However, we don't want to offend the collectors. Go to the lake and throw in a hook and line. Open the mouth of the first fish that you catch, and you will find a denarius. Take it and give it to the tax collectors for me and yourself."

Once more Judas' secret was safe from the rest of the apostles.

It was late afternoon when Peter returned from paying the temple tax. The Group was assembled in his courtyard. Jesus sat on a low stool and the others were sitting on their haunches in a semicircle.

"Come on in the house. Hachilah is probably preparing supper for us," Peter invited, but could tell by the look on Jesus' face that Jesus had something important to say, and had been awaiting his return. He found a place and joined the others in the semicircle.

"What were you arguing about along the way?" Jesus asked. Peter, who was never at a loss for words, said nothing. Neither did Judas, which was not unusual, since he was mostly quiet and unobtrusive. The silence was that of a group of little boys caught in a forbidden prank. When it became obvious that no one was going to say anything, Jesus called to Peter's four-year-old son, "Jonathan, come here." Jonathan eagerly slipped into the circle and snuggled into Jesus' arms.

"Unless you repent of your sins and become as a little child, you'll not even get into the Kingdom of Heaven. If you humble yourself and become as this little child, you will be the greatest in the Kingdom of Heaven. It would be better for you to have a millstone tied around your neck and thrown into the lake than to betray the trust of one of these little ones."

"The world is full of trouble because of all the temptations. Trials and troubles will come, but it will be especially bad for him who is the instrument of trouble. He would have been better off if he had never been born."

Judas had the impression that this last statement was meant for him, but he hadn't offended any little kid unless Jesus meant Peter, an awfully big kid. He had about had it with Peter.

Peter changed the subject. "How often should I forgive my brother?" he asked. "Seven times?"

Jesus replied, "Not just seven times, but seventy times seven."

CHAPTER 20

ELIHU

Elihu was elated. He finally had enough money to buy that house on the hill that he had wanted for so long. Now he could marry Rachel. They had planned long ago to marry when he could afford a house. All the arrangements had been made by their parents while he and Rachel were small children. It was a natural choice, since Elihu's father and Rachel's father were scribes.

As a lad, Elihu had been privileged to go with his father into the House of Rolls. His father would take one of the scrolls that had become brittle with age and use.

"Father, what are you going to do with the scroll?" Elihu expressed his childhood curiosity.

"I have to copy on new papyrus," his father had patiently replied. "This one is old and brittle."

Then his father would put the scroll on a special easel to hold it. Turning the left spindle, he rolled the scroll into the canister until he came to the book's beginning. Sitting on a stool at a sloping desk upon which a fresh papyrus was unrolled, he would take a reed pen dipped in ink, and starting at the upper right hand corner, he would carefully copy the Hebrew letters in vertical columns.

"How do you know what they say, Father?" Elihu had asked in childhood inquisitiveness.

"When you have finished your lessons with Rabbi Abiathar, you will know what they say."

"You mean like in phylacteries?"

"That and much more. You will know all the Law and The Prophets."

From that day on in the House of Rolls, Elihu never lost his fascination for the Holy Scriptures. He did learn from Rabbi Abiathar to read and write and to copy and interpret the Torah accurately.

Now, he worked alongside his father in the House of Rolls. Although he did not judge the Law, his services in instructing pupils paid well. He had earned enough to buy a house, and he and Rachel could marry as soon as he returned from the feast at Jerusalem. His father had gone before to make arrangements for the feast, and he had stayed behind to make legal arrangements for his house.

The legal arrangements took longer than he had anticipated, and he missed the main party of pilgrims going down to Jerusalem for the feast. It was too dangerous to go down to Jerusalem alone because of the robbers who lurked along the roads.

Elihu began to inquire about a later party going to the feast. He went to the home of his friend Aaron, who sometimes went with another party. A servant named Benzoheth answered the gate. "My lord, Aaron, has already gone with the main party to Jerusalem, but I hear that some people are going down with the party of Jesus of Nazareth."

"Thank you. Which way did they go?"

"They started down the road toward Samaria."

"Are you sure? Jews don't go through Samaria."

"I know it sounds crazy, but that is the way they went. If you hurry, you can catch them."

Elihu had heard of Jesus of Nazareth, and if everything that had been said about him were true, Jesus could very well be the Messiah. He knew that none of the rulers believed it, but they only studied the scrolls they liked and even those they interpreted to suit their own ideas. Some even threatened him when he didn't interpret the Scriptures to agree with their whims, but he loved the Scriptures too much to twist the obvious meaning. Now was a good time to find out for himself who Jesus really was.

He hurried down the road toward Samaria at a brisk walk. It was as Benzoheth had said. As he rounded a curve in the road, he could see a band of people in the valley below him. They had stopped, and two men were coming toward them from the opposite direction. He ran toward the group and arrived at about the same time that the two men did.

"Teacher, we went to the village . . . to find a place to stay tonight, . . . but when they found . . . that we were on our way to Jerusalem, . . . they refused . . . and demanded that we get out of Samaria!" Judas, out of breath from running and agitation, spoke haltingly. He and Simon had gone ahead to make eating and sleeping arrangements for the Group.

James and John crowded around Jesus like two eager children. "Teacher, shall we call fire down from heaven and burn them up like Elijah, the prophet, did?"

"No! You don't know of what sort of spirit you are. The Son of Man didn't come to destroy men's lives, but to save them."

They crossed Jordan and took the route of the earlier pilgrims.

As Elihu listened to Jesus' teaching and saw his miracles, he became more impressed that Jesus was the Messiah. That night as he lay in the courtyard of Amnon and Damaris, a Jewish family whose son he had taught the Holy Scriptures, he pondered all that he had seen and heard that day. Amnon and Damaris were disciples of Jesus and had taken Elihu aside after a bountiful meal and told him of the joy of believing Jesus and the new life they had found.

Elihu was piqued by their assuming the role of teacher while he found himself a pupil, but as they described their experiences and Jesus' miracles and teaching, the Scriptures that he had puzzled over became clear, and he became convinced that Jesus was indeed the Messiah. But, did he want to follow Jesus? The rulers at Jerusalem had threatened to throw anyone out of the synagogue who followed Jesus; however, the rulers at Capernaum had asked Jesus to speak in their synagogue. Elihu decided that he had nothing to fear. He was a scribe, as was his father.

Amnon and Damaris still attended the synagogue. He would do it. Elihu decided to tell Jesus in the morning. Having made a firm decision, his mind was free of turmoil and he slept.

The next morning, Elihu could hardly wait to tell Jesus that he wanted to be a disciple, too. "Teacher, I will go with you wherever you go!" He was certain that Jesus would be glad to have a scribe for a disciple.

"Foxes have holes, and birds have nests, but the Son of Man doesn't have a place to lay his head," Jesus said, and continued on his way.

Elihu was stunned. What kind of answer was that? He had offered his services and been rebuffed.

"Are you a new disciple?" Judas asked. He had seen Elihu join the party yesterday.

"Well, I'd thought I'd be, but I don't think your teacher wants me."

"Why do you say that?"

"'Foxes have holes and birds have nests, but the Son of Man doesn't have any place to lay his head' doesn't sound like an answer of encouragement to me."

"Do you own any property?" Judas asked.

"Well, yes, I just bought a house yesterday," Elihu replied.

"You will have to sell it and give the money to the poor." Judas saw a chance to fill the bag once more.

"But I bought this house so I could get married."

Judas didn't press any further and Elihu dropped back to the rear of the party, concluding that he had offered his services and Jesus had refused. The party with which they were traveling arrived in Jerusalem the next day.

Jesus chose seventy disciples and sent them on tour. Judas went with them. After they had gone, Elihu began to again consider becoming a disciple. Judas had said that he would need to sell his house, but if Jesus really were the Messiah, he couldn't let a house keep him out of the Kingdom. Jesus had emphasized eternal life. He would find out just what a person would have to do to inherit eternal life. With that in mind, he found Jesus teaching a small group of disciples that had not been chosen to go out with the Seventy.

Approaching Jesus, he said, "Teacher, just what do I need to do to inherit eternal life?"

"You know what the Law says; how do you interpret it?"

Elihu thought, "I guess Jesus recognizes my knowledge of the

Law after all." He had summarized the Law many times for his students. All the Law hinged on two commandments. "You shall love the Lord your God with all your heart and with all your soul and with all your mind and with all your strength, and your neighbor as yourself."

"You are correct. Do this and you will have eternal life."

Elihu was surprised. He hadn't expected Jesus to agree with him. No more of this "Foxes have holes, and birds have nests" nonsense. Jesus hadn't said anything about selling his house. But, wait a minute. The man who was standing at his elbow in the crowd was a Samaritan. Elihu had seen him join the party when he had caught up with them in Samaria. Jesus surely wouldn't expect anyone to love a Samaritan; they didn't even have souls. Just to be sure, he asked Jesus, "Who is my neighbor?"

"There was a certain man who left Jerusalem to go to Jericho on business one morning. On his way, robbers caught him, beat him, took his money and left him to die. A little later in the day, a priest came by, saw him, and passed by on the other side of the road. Still later, a Levite came by. The Levite stopped and looked at the man lying in the gully groaning. Then he turned away and walked on down the road."

Elihu remembered a day when he was a young scribe. His father had suggested that he go to Jerusalem to study the Scriptures there. There was one scroll at Jericho that he needed to copy. He remembered seeing a man in a ditch on his way to Jericho. He felt sorry for him, but he had never seen the man before. Since he didn't know him, he wasn't a neighbor. Therefore, he was under no obligation to help him. Jesus couldn't have known about it since the man was not conscious and Elihu was alone.

Jesus continued his story: "Some time later, a Samaritan came that way. He dismounted from his donkey, bound up the victim's wounds, put him on his donkey and took him to an inn. He gave the innkeeper two weeks rent and told him to take care of the man until he was well. He promised to pay the innkeeper for any more expense when he came back that way. Which of these three men was neighbor to the victim of the robbery?"

Elihu felt very uncomfortable. All eyes were turned in his direction. There was no way that any of them could know that he was the Levite passing on the road that day. Besides, the priest should have been neighbor to the man. He was from Jerusalem. He may have even known who he was. Elihu had spent all his life in Capernaum, except for the brief time that he had studied in Jerusalem. There was no way that he was obligated to that man in the ditch. Yet Jesus expected an answer. Elihu looked at the Samaritan standing at his side. That man, too, was expecting an answer. He could tell by the expression on the Samaritan's face that he was not the man who had taken care of the victim. On the other hand, neither he nor the priest had shown any neighborly love toward the unfortunate man in the gully.

"I suppose it was the one who showed mercy toward the wounded man," Elihu grudgingly admitted.

"Go and do likewise," Jesus advised.

Elihu elbowed his way through the crowd. He had never been so humiliated in his life. No wonder the scribes and Pharisees at Jerusalem wanted to kill Jesus. He would like to kill him himself. He would go to the Temple, where he was appreciated.

"Elihu! We have been expecting you five days ago." Japhia, a fellow scribe of Jerusalem, greeted him. He had met Japhia when he was studying at Jerusalem. They had become fast friends, and they renewed acquaintance every year at the Feast.

As soon as they had inquired about the health of each other's families, Elihu explained his tardiness. "I bought a house from old Hagab, and I was afraid that if I didn't complete the transaction before I came down to Jerusalem, he would sell it to someone else."

"That sounds like something that old grasshopper would do," chuckled Japhia.

"By the time we had met with the elders at the gate, the main party had left Capernaum. I came down with the Jesus of Nazareth party."

"You are not a disciple of the Nazarene, are you?" Japhia interrupted.

"Oh, no, I wouldn't have anything to do with that madman. I just came with the party for protection from bandits along the road."

"That was good thinking. I heard they robbed old Iddo. He started out ahead of the main party. Luckily, they found him the next day. He was still black and blue when he arrived here. But, as for this Jesus of Nazareth, the chief priests have already decided to kill him, but he hasn't shown up in Jerusalem yet."

"I would like to kill him myself, but he hasn't done anything to break the Law." Elihu was still smarting from the humiliation that he imagined he had received. He could imagine how that ugly Samaritan was gloating. He wondered why he had even considered following Jesus.

"Maybe he hasn't done anything to break the Law, but for a price two witnesses can always be found to condemn a man whether he is guilty or not," Japhia broke into Judas' thoughts. "All we need to do is get him away from the crowds."

Elihu was startled. Japhia was in on the conspiracy (a conspiracy it was). Had he followed his inclination to join the Nazarene cult, he would be in big trouble. There was no doubt that his friendship would not have kept Japhia from turning him over to the authorities.

"By the way, perhaps you may know someone in that Group who could help us catch Jesus."

"I wasn't with the party long enough to get acquainted with any of the disciples. The majority were just like me, traveling with the group for protection."

Elihu was frightened. Just what kind of man was Japhia. They had been close friends, but somehow he was seeing a side of him that he didn't know at all.

"They tell me that Jesus has an inner circle of disciples that are trained in the mysteries of the kingdom," Japhia continued as though he hadn't heard Elihu's disclaimer. "I suspect that there is someone in that group who would sell out."

"I haven't the slightest idea of what you are saying."

"Yes, you do. You'll think of someone when the time is right."

CHAPTER 21

THE GREAT GULF

Judas and Simon were very tired. They had been gone three months, traveling from village to village in Judea. It had been a thrilling three months. They had missed the Feast of Tabernacles. It was half over when Jesus had sent seventy out in teams of two. Maybe they would be in time for the Feast of Dedication. At any rate, they would have success to report.

In every village they had been received with joy. It seemed as though the people had been expecting them. The preaching, the healing, even the exorcising of devils had been accomplished with ease and freedom, as though it was the normal and natural thing to do. They had been aware of a supernatural power that carried them through the days and weeks. And now they were approaching Jerusalem. Many other people were approaching Jerusalem, too.

The road from Jericho ascended steadily toward Jerusalem. As they rounded a curve, the panorama of Jerusalem lay before them. The evening sun glistened on the spires of the Temple; even the Tower of Antonia was softened in the sunlight.

"What a beautiful city!" Simon exclaimed involuntarily.

Judas agreed, "Yes, there is none like it in all the world. It is the City of David and the City of God."

"Do you think that Jesus will claim the throne?" Simon asked.

"Elihu, the scribe, says that Jesus has every right to it. He traced his lineage through Joseph back to King David."

"Elihu? Is that the man who wanted to join the Group and then changed his mind when Jesus told him that he would be homeless? The Kingdom is no place for half-heartedness."

"He may still join after he has had time to think things through."

"Yes, Jesus wants his followers to know what hardships befall those who follow him. I don't think I would follow a mere king."

Simon's statement surprised Judas. "What do you mean, 'a mere king?'"

"I believe that Jesus is the Son of God."

"Don't say that! That's blasphemy!"

"King David didn't walk on water, heal the sick, still the storm and raise . . ."

Simon was sounding so convincing that Judas changed the subject. "Look at the crowd down there!" he said. There before them was a great crowd of people almost filling the Kidron Valley. Simon and Judas stood in amazement. They could hear a voice, but were too far away to understand the words. Jesus was standing by the city wall speaking to the people in the valley. He used the city wall as a natural amplifier to fill the valley with his hearty booming voice. His articulation was so perfect that the farthest person in the crowd heard clearly.

That familiar voice was a welcome sound to Judas and Simon. The tour had been much more successful than their prior one. They had been welcome in every town and village, and although extremely tired, they were eager to tell Jesus of their triumph.

The voice stopped. The crowd started moving through the Eastern gate before it closed at sunset. The gate closed before Judas and Simon arrived, and they faced the prospect of spending the night in the damp, cold Kidron Valley.

"Let's go to the Garden of Gethsemane," Simon suggested. "Jesus and the rest will come there for prayer."

Before Judas could answer, a man stepped out of the shadows. "Hail, Judas, I haven't seen you for three months," Elihu said. Judas returned the greeting, but was aloof until he was sure of Elihu's intentions.

"Come over to my house and spend the night. I sold my house in Capernaum, but I didn't give the proceeds to the poor. I bought a house here in Jerusalem. Come on, we can still go through the

North gate. I doubt that it will be closed tonight. It's usually left open during feast days."

Judas agreed to go with Elihu, but Simon declined, saying he wanted to report their tour to Jesus that night.

When they arrived at Elihu's house, Elihu commanded a servant to wash Judas' feet. Later, the servant brought bread and veal and set it before Judas. Judas was hungry and grateful to his host for the food.

"Your teacher, Jesus, has been causing some problems since you've been gone," Elihu began.

"Yes, how is that?" Judas answered warily, for he suspected that Elihu had an ulterior motive in inviting him to his home.

"What I am going to tell you is for your best interests and for your teacher. I do think that Jesus might have a legal claim to the throne, but if he doesn't stop offending our religious leaders, he is going to get himself killed. If I were you, I would warn him; and if he won't listen, get out yourself, because they may kill his disciples, too."

"Why do you think the rulers are going to kill Jesus?"

"Weren't you here during the Feast of the Tabernacles?" Elihu had assumed that Judas was present since they had been traveling in the same party to the feast.

"No, Jesus sent us on tour the day before."

"On the last day of the feast after the pouring out of the water, Jesus said that anyone wanting to drink could come to him as though he were the Messiah. To make matters worse, he told the Jews who challenged him that they were children of the devil, not Abraham. And get this—he claimed that he was alive before Abraham. Needless to say, it was clearly blasphemy and the rulers were furious."

"I know that the rulers would like to kill Jesus; he knows it, too. But as for carrying out the threat, that is impossible. No one can kill a man like Jesus. I have seen him walk on water, and I have seen him speak to a storm and it stopped immediately. He is a prophet like Elijah, and fire from heaven may fall on those who try to kill him."

"I never thought of that," Elihu said. He was awed. "What about this 'Son of God' idea?"

"Peter believes that he is the Son of God, and Simon just told me that he did."

"How about you, what do you believe?"

"As I told you before, I believe he is a prophet like Elijah and Elisha, nothing more." Judas had a sinking feeling that he had talked too freely. He didn't quite trust Elihu. When Elihu suggested that they retire for the night, he was relieved.

CHAPTER 22

DEATH OF A FRIEND

Judas chafed under the seemingly fruitless routine. They were going to the same villages and towns that he and Simon visited before. Jesus was teaching about the Kingdom of Heaven as if there was going to be a kingdom. Jesus had already passed up two opportunities to be king, once when he had fed that crowd on the other side of Lake Galilee. They were ready to march with him to Jerusalem. And, according to Elihu, he claimed to be the Messiah at the Feast of Dedication. If he really wanted to be King, instead of preaching, he should have shown his power with some kind of miracle then.

It seemed that they had been here at Bethany beyond Jordan a month. Judas liked to keep moving. All those parables that Jesus taught didn't make sense. He didn't understand them and didn't care.

His boredom was broken by someone coming on the road from Jerusalem. As the person came nearer, he could make out that the skirts of his garment were tied at the waist and that he was running.

A messenger! Judas moved from the outer edge of the crowd closer to Jesus and the rest of the Twelve to hear what the messenger was saying.

"Teacher . . . your friend . . . Lazarus is sick . . . and my mistress, Martha, . . . wants you to come and heal him," Ami said between gulps of air.

"This sickness is not unto death. It is for God's glory, and God's son may be glorified through it," Jesus said.

It was now sunset and Ami stayed with the disciples that night. He had delivered the message, and Jesus had said that Lazarus wouldn't die, so there was no urgency to return to Bethany.

When the morning came, Judas expected Jesus to go back to Judea and heal Lazarus, but instead he sent Ami away and began teaching the people in parables again. He remembered that Jesus had healed the Roman Centurion's slave from a distance; in all probability, Ami would find Lazarus healed when he returned to Bethany in Judea.

They stayed at Bethany beyond Jordan that day and the next. At the end of the second day, Jesus called the Twelve apart. "Tomorrow we are going back to Judea"

"But teacher, the last time we were there, the Jews tried to stone you. You surely aren't going back?" Peter was the spokesman, but the rest joined in protest.

"There are twelve hours in a day. A man can walk in the day and not stumble," Jesus said. "Our friend Lazarus has gone to sleep. I am going back to Bethany to wake him up."

"If he is asleep, he will get better," James said.

"Lazarus is dead. For your sakes I am glad that I was not there when he died, because now you will believe. Let's go to him."

"Let's all go with him so that we may die with him," Thomas Didymous said.

Judas thought to himself, "You can speak for yourself, Thomas, but I don't want to die with him." However, Judas didn't want to be left alone in Bethany beyond Jordan. After all, Jesus could perform a miracle and protect them all.

CHAPTER 23

YOUR BROTHER SHALL RISE AGAIN

When Ami arrived back in Bethany, he was stunned to learn that Lazarus was dead. "It took much longer than I thought," he told Martha.

"Oh, Ami, don't blame yourself. Lazarus died the very day you left," Martha said, comforting her slave. "We had no way of calling you back, and Jesus couldn't have known."

"I don't understand. Jesus said that my master would not die. I could have come back sooner if I had known that he was dead."

"Jesus may have meant that Lazarus would not have died if he had been here. We should have sent for him sooner. We knew that Lazarus was very sick. You did all you could do." Martha burst into tears and gathered Ami into her arms. Grief erased the master-slave relationship, and they wept together for the loss of one they both loved.

After their tears had subsided, Ami went back to his duties as a slave. He still felt great sorrow that Lazarus was gone, but he knew Martha didn't blame him for what had happened. A slave has only to obey his master. He can't be troubled by things he doesn't understand.

Martha went back into the house where the hired mourners were wailing and quoting comforting scripture verses. There would be two more days of mourning. Afterward, there would be a thirty-day period before normal activities would resume.

Martha had tried to give Lazarus a decent burial. Mary had been so overcome with grief that she was practically helpless. Poor thing. Lazarus had been the big brother and she the little sister, tagging after him as he tilled the fields.

"Mary, Lazarus knew that he would die someday. That is why he had the tomb enlarged behind the garden. There is room for you and me; we will die, too, someday." Martha was always the practical one.

"But he was still young," Mary sobbed. "Not old like Abba and Mamma. I just know that if Jesus had been here, he wouldn't have died."

"I know, but Jesus can't be every place at one time," Martha tried to explain to Mary. "If he had stayed at Jerusalem, he might have been killed himself. Tabeel said that the rulers tried to stone him at the Feast."

"You're right," Mary said. "But it seems like a bad dream for Lazarus to be gone. I wish we had sent for Jesus sooner. We knew Lazarus was sick. He had been sick all winter."

Martha felt a twinge of guilt. What Mary was saying was true, but some days he was better. She had kept hoping that he would recover. Last week his condition worsened. The sun was setting at the beginning of the Sabbath when she had become alarmed at his condition. His face and hands were hot to the touch and he became delirious. As soon as the Sabbath was over, she had sent Ami to find Jesus.

However, Martha knew that her sister was not reproaching her, but it was deep grief for her dead brother, the brother who had teased her and become a second abba when "abba" and "mamma" had died fifteen years ago in a plague.

Martha, as the eldest, had assumed the family leadership. Lazarus had been a mere lad of fifteen and Mary had been only a toddler. Lazarus assumed the field work and took Mary with him. He would gird the skirts of her garments up like a boy's and let her ride the little donkey while he goaded the oxen along. Martha chided him about it, but the two were inseparable.

They were not a wealthy family, but were able to live comfortably. Their only slave was Ami, who drove the other team of oxen when Lazarus tilled the fields.

Even in her grief, practical-minded Martha was thinking ahead. They might have to hire another slave. No, that would never do. Ami worked hard and was obedient, but couldn't manage a farm. Mary might. She wasn't much help with the housework. Jesus had said at one time, when he had been their guest, that learning spiritual things was more important than doing housework. Of course, that was true, but housework had to be done. Perhaps Mary and Ami could work in the fields, and she would do the housework alone. Mary was old enough to have a husband. Lazarus should have made arrangements with some young man's parents for Mary to marry. Well, it was her responsibility now. Mary had never given any indication of being attracted to any of the local young men. When the mourning period was over, she would attend to the matter.

"May the Lord of Consolation comfort you! Blessed is he who comforts the mourners!" One of the hired mourners was practically shouting in her ear. Martha wished that they would go away. They weren't comforting her. They had come as soon as Lazarus died, and they had kept up a constant din ever since. They had only come for the pay that they would get when the four days of mourning were past. That would be at sundown today.

Ami appeared at the gate. Martha welcomed the interruption as she went to hear his message.

"The teacher is here," Ami said.

"Where is he?"

"He is at the garden."

Martha followed Ami to the garden that the family owned at the edge of the village. It was in a cave at the back of this garden where her parents were buried and where Lazarus' body had been laid. Jesus and the Twelve were standing at the garden entrance waiting for her.

"Lord, if you had been here, my brother would not have died. And I know that even now, whatever you ask of God, he will give it to you." The presence of Jesus brought a fresh outburst of grief, and Martha fell at his feet sobbing.

"Your brother will rise again," Jesus said.

"I know that he will rise again in the resurrection at the last day," Martha said.

"I am the resurrection and life."

What Jesus was saying didn't make sense to Martha. "I had better go get Mary," she thought. "She understands those great mysteries that he teaches." She went back to the house and said to Mary, "The teacher is here and he is asking for you."

Mary hurried after Martha, and the mourners followed, thinking that she was going to the tomb to mourn. Martha had not gone back to the tomb since the funeral four days ago, but Mary had gone often. It seemed to comfort her to be near Lazarus' final resting place. Jesus was waiting for them.

"Lord if you had been here, my brother would not have died," Mary sobbed, not as a reproach, but as an outcry of grief.

Unlike the hired mourners, genuinely concerned friends and neighbors wept openly and brokenly. Watching in a detached way, Judas did not feel their sorrow. Lazarus was a good, old boy, but Judas hadn't felt too comfortable when they had stayed at Martha's house before. They were just too holy. Evidently, Lazarus hadn't been too ambitious because, instead of taking a wife, he had stayed with Martha and Mary after his parents died.

Judas didn't know why Mary wasn't betrothed. He guessed she was too lazy and homely for any man to want. Martha's husband had died in the same plague that took her parents. He didn't understand why Jesus had come back to Bethany. Lazarus was already dead, and the mourning period was almost over. The mourners would go home tonight.

"Your teacher is crying, too." A voice at Judas' elbow startled him. It was Elihu.

"Where are they going?" Elihu pointed toward Jesus and the two women moving through the trees toward the back of the garden.

Judas didn't answer but followed the crowd. As they walked along, Elihu filled Judas in with the latest details of the activities of the scribes and the Pharisees. Elihu considered Judas a friend because he wasn't as fanatical as the rest of the group.

"Did you know that the leaders are going to try to kill Jesus?"

"Yes, I heard they wanted to. Some of the disciples didn't want him to come back to Jerusalem for that reason."

"He should have listened to them. All the rulers need is to catch him alone; they can't arrest him with all the people around. It might start a riot, and the Romans would wipe us out."

"That won't happen. He is never alone, except at night when he is praying."

"Where does he go to pray?" Elihu's question alerted Judas.

"Why would you want to know unless . . . ?" Judas stopped, realizing that it might sound like an accusation.

"Unless I wanted him caught." Elihu finished the sentence for Judas. "I know that I considered joining your group at one time, but it is too dangerous to join now. If you are wise, you will leave the Nazarene party while you can. The rulers have decided that Jesus must be stopped, and they will do it one way or another."

"You underestimate Jesus. He can heal; feed five thousand people; stop a storm . . ." Judas didn't get to finish the sentence. The crowd stopped in front of the tomb at the back of Martha's garden.

"What are they doing?" Elihu pointed to two men who were rolling the stone away from the tomb's entrance.

They heard Jesus praying, but were too far way to understand the words of the prayer. Yet they heard the next words clearly, "Lazarus. Come out!"

A figure appeared in the doorway, bound in grave clothes. "Take the grave clothes off him and let him go," Jesus said.

Judas had been going to explain to Elihu that no one could kill someone who could raise the dead, but Elihu was already running in the direction of Jerusalem to tell what had happened.

"Come, let us be going." Jesus had separated himself from the crowd that had gathered around Lazarus after the grave clothes had been taken off and a cloak had been thrown over him. The Twelve followed Jesus without another word.

As they passed through Jerusalem, they saw a new house on a hill.

"Look," said Simon. "That is Elihu's new house. You remember, he was the scribe who was going to follow Jesus until Jesus said that foxes have holes and birds have nests, but the Son of Man has no place to lay his head. I hear he sold his house in Capernaum and bought this one just last week."

Judas made no comment, but Matthew said, "This may be one of those times that we will have no place to lay our heads."

Matthew's remark proved to be true. They crossed the Kidron Brook about sunset and found a small cave a short distance from the road and built a fire. They went to sleep hungry that night because they hadn't taken time to buy anything to eat.

It was fortunate for Judas that they hadn't. The bag was empty again. People were giving small sums, but it was never enough to meet all their needs. They were always having to spend it for food. Judas had hoped they could stay overnight at Martha's house. The Bethany home always fed them well and filled their baskets before they left, but he couldn't blame Jesus for wanting to get out of Judea as soon as possible. He had no doubt that Elihu was right that the Jewish rulers would try to kill Jesus at the first opportunity. But how could you kill someone who could raise the dead?

CHAPTER 24

CEDRON

Cedron was sad. He didn't have much future. Not since those reddish brown spots had appeared on his face. When they appeared on his ears, his hands and his buttocks, he had left home. His wife had wanted him to show himself to the priest, but he didn't need a priest to tell him that he had leprosy.

He had gone outside the city, Bethshan Scythopolis, because he didn't want to expose any of his family, friends or neighbors to his horrible disease. He had planned to just starve, but after a day or two of not eating, his instinct for survival prevailed and he found himself slipping up to the wall at night and digging through the garbage that had been thrown through the dung gate.

What few scraps of food he found were spoiled, and after one or two bouts with food poisoning he abandoned that source. Instead, he learned to go through the ripening grain fields and pick off a few heads. By rubbing them together between his palms and blowing the chaff away he would have a handful to eat.

Aside from the sores that festered, burst and dried up, leaving a sunken spot in his face, Cedron had no pain. He managed to keep alive until the barley harvest was over, the last sheaf had been gathered, and the poor had gleaned.

Without purpose, plan or hope Cedron had wondered farther away from his hometown of Bethshan in Samaria. In a few short weeks he had descended from a prominent head of a family to a thieving scavenger. Thoughts of starvation had been replaced with the will to survive.

He didn't try to worship God, whatever god the Samaritans worshipped. They worshipped on every high hill and in the groves. He soon learned that the sacrifice was good to eat if one could get it soon after the worshipper left. Before he had contracted this awful disease, he would have been afraid that God would kill him, but now he hoped He would.

Leprosy has no borders. Cedron slept in his rags where he happened to be when night came, and he was not aware that he had crossed the border into Galilee. Morning came and he arose to another day of aimless wandering. He rounded a turn in the path and came face to face with a party of Galileeans.

"Unclean! Unclean!" he shouted automatically. He tried to keep out of the way of well people, but if one did happen to meet a well person and didn't yell, "unclean," one might get clubbed or stoned.

"Don't worry, we're unclean, too. My name is Hattil. You're welcome to join our group," Hattil said, although as a Jew, he would have shunned Cedron, a Samaritan, but tragedy sweeps away all racial and social barriers.

Hattil led the way to a makeshift camp in a little valley where a small stream gurgled. There were four small tents made of scraps of goat skins that they had managed to steal. Hattil's tent was complete. He had managed to steal it from an Arab while he was sleeping in it. This had given him clear leadership of the group.

"You will have to steal your own tent," Hattil said. "We only allow two to a tent." Clearly, Hattil had no intentions of sharing his tent, although it was larger than all the rest.

Cedron shivered through the night. After sunrise, the sun soon warmed him. The rest of the lepers were still in their tents. It was not until the sun was high enough to make it uncomfortably warm in their tents that they came out. There was no food. Nothing to do but forage.

They shuffled along toward Ephraim, where one of the group had gleaned last week. There was not much hope of finding anything because the farmers were preparing and sowing their fields for the spring harvest.

Someone had accidentally spilled a few seeds on the path. They all got down on their knees until they had found and eaten every grain.

As they continued on their way toward Ephraim, Hattil suddenly stopped. "There is a crowd of people coming toward us," he said.

"Who is it?" asked Amzi, the leper whose tent was next to Hattil's.

"Shall we yell 'unclean'?" asked Gibbar, the leper who shared Amzi's tent.

"Maybe we ought to run," said Binen, the leper who was friendlier with Cedron than the rest.

As the crowd drew nearer, Cedron recognized the figure in the front. He had seen him when he visited his sister at Sychar two years ago. It was Jesus of Nazareth. His sister had become a disciple, but, although he had been impressed by Jesus, he had not been ready to follow him.

"It is Jesus of Nazareth," Cedron said.

"You mean the great healer!" Hattil exclaimed. "Maybe he will heal us. Jesus, master, have mercy on us!" he yelled, and the rest joined in.

"Go show yourself to the priest," Jesus answered.

They all turned and hobbled away as fast as their crippled feet would allow them. As Cedron ran, he realized that he wasn't hobbling anymore. He stopped and looked at his hands. They were no longer twisted stubs. He felt his face. No nodules of blood and pus. He was healed! He was no longer a leper. He felt a great wave of gratitude well up in his heart. He watched as his companions in misery disappeared over the brow of a hill. He was aware of the crowd approaching from behind. He turned and shouted, "Praise God, I'm healed! I'm not a leper anymore. O, thank you. Thank you, Lord!"

Jesus asked the crowd, "Were there not ten cleansed? Where are the other nine? Wasn't anyone thankful enough to praise God, except this Samaritan?" Then Jesus said to Cedron, "Get up and go. Your faith has made you well."

Judas was bored with the whole thing. He used to be excited

about Jesus' miracles, but after seeing Lazarus come out of the tomb, what was exciting about healing a few lepers? Even miracles were becoming "ho hum" to him, and he wasn't even sure that he wanted an important place in the kingdom anymore.

If Jesus had only given Elihu more encouragement. That young man had a lot of influence with the rulers. Otherwise, he couldn't have had that fancy house on the hill.

What was it that Elihu had said, "If they could catch Jesus when the crowd wasn't around?" Maybe that was the answer. No, he wouldn't let himself think about it. On the other hand, Jesus needed to be forced into using his miraculous power to make himself a king. He surely had as much power as the prophets of old. Elijah had called fire down from heaven on fifty men that King Ahaziah had sent. Elisha had blinded the eyes of the whole Aramean army.

CHAPTER 25

ON THE JERICHO ROAD

The laughter of little children in the morning air aroused Judas from sleep. They had joined a party of pilgrims yesterday on the way to Jerusalem to observe the Passover. Judas had not been too well pleased by the unusual number of children in the party. Their incessant chatter, screaming and general boisterousness got on his nerves. Their parents didn't seem to care and never rebuked them unless they got into a fight. Even after they had settled down for the night, Judas had trouble sleeping. Now, here they were beginning again.

Jesus was sitting on the ground talking to them as though they were as important as adults. Their parents were standing around doing nothing. Judas was exasperated. "You children go away and let the teacher alone," he said.

"Allow the children to come to me," Jesus said. "The Kingdom of God belongs to them."

Judas couldn't believe what he was hearing. Jesus was going to accept children into the Kingdom. That settled it. He didn't want any part of a kingdom of children.

As they approached Jericho, another party of pilgrims from Capernaum caught up with them.

"It's Mother!" John and James said at the same time. She was alone and Judas wondered where old Zebedee was. Probably fishing. What Judas didn't know was that Zebedee had drowned in a boating accident. One of those sudden storms had hit the lake one night and capsized his boat. His body had washed ashore three days later. There hadn't been any time for a funeral because of the deteriorating condition of the body. James and John were with Jesus at the raising of Lazarus that day. Although the widow, Salome, was still in mourning, she had come down with the party from Capernaum to tell her sons about it. Instead of going into paroxysms of grief over the news, they persuaded her to ask Jesus for a special privilege.

"What is it you want?" Jesus asked.

"Grant that one of these two sons of mine sit at your right hand and the other at your left in your Kingdom," Salome asked. James and John were standing behind her, waiting to hear Jesus' response.

"You have no idea what you are asking," Jesus said, and looking at the men, he continued, "Can you drink the cup that I am going to drink?"

"We can," they answered.

"You will, indeed, drink from my cup, but to sit at my left or right is not mine to grant. These places will be given to those whom my Father chooses."

The very nerve of those sons of Zebedee. They not only wanted the chief places in the Kingdom, but they had used their own mother to try to get it and she in mourning. Although Judas had already decided that he wanted no part in a kingdom that included children, he was furious with James and John and their unbridled ambition. He was not the only one. Peter, Matthew and Simon began to upbraid James and John. "Why do you think you are more qualified for the job than the rest of us?"

Jesus patiently called them aside and said, "You know that the rulers of the Gentiles lord it over their subjects. That is not the way it's going to be with you. Instead, whoever wants to be great among you must be your slave. And whoever wants to be first must take the least position, just as the Son of Man did not come to be served, but to serve and to give his life for many."

Kingdom or no kingdom, Judas didn't plan to be anyone's slave.

CHAPTER 26

ZACCHAEUS

Zacchaeus was elated. Jesus was actually going to come to his house. He had heard about the Nazarene who could throw out devils, heal disease, still storms, feed five thousand people with a little bread and two small fish. And he had heard about Lazarus being raised from the dead. He wanted to see this great person. When someone had told him that Jesus would be passing through Jericho on his way to Jerusalem, he had closed his tax booth with the hope of seeing him. However, he had a problem; he was only four feet, nine inches tall. There was no way that he could see over the crowd.

All of his life he had been teased and slighted because of his small stature. Now his lack of height was preventing him from seeing the person he most wanted to see in the world.

But difficulties had never deterred Zacchaeus for long. He had not become a chief tax collector by letting problems defeat him. He knew there was a sycamore fig growing beside the road on the other side of Jericho. He took a back street and soon passed the crowd. He climbed up in the leafy branches of the tree and found a branch overlooking the road. There he waited until the crowd was directly underneath the branch. They entered and passed through Jericho. Suddenly, Jesus stopped and looked up into the fig tree and said, "Zacchaeus, come down immediately. I must stay at your house today."

When Zacchaeus shinnied down the tree, Judas felt the anger rising in his heart. He remembered that lying little b—d. He got Judas in trouble with the Romans. He had told them that Judas had not turned over all the tax money he had collected at Jericho. He had laughed when Judas had been forced to replace the supposed shortage out of his own funds. Jesus was going to be a guest in that man's house! Enough was enough. He didn't want any more to do with a kingdom of little children, big-headed fishermen and crooked tax collectors. No matter that he himself had been a tax collector; he had never betrayed a man in his own business.

Judas left the crowd and went on to Jerusalem. He found the big house on the hill and approached Elihu's gate.

Zacchaeus was so excited about Jesus' words that he didn't wonder how Jesus knew his name nor why he was in the tree. It had been a long time since anyone had used his right name.

He was usually called "shorty" or "runt." He was shunned by all the rabbis and scribes and priests in Jericho. Of course, he knew when he took the job that he would be an outcast. It didn't matter. He was rich and he had obtained his riches legitimately.

He only charged poor people what the Roman government required plus a little bit to cover expenses, but the scribes and Pharisees could afford more. He charged them all he could get by with, and that was plenty because he had the Roman army behind him. They could call him names behind his back, but they didn't dare say it to his face.

He really didn't know why he wanted to see Jesus, but since he had heard about him, he had felt a restless longing. Now Jesus was sitting in his house, eating his food and treating him like a real person. Nevertheless, all the lying, cheating and stealing was weighing on his heart.

He stood up and motioned to all the disciples at his table and the onlookers in the courtyard, "If I have cheated anybody, I will repay him four times as much, and I am going to give half of all I own to the poor."

Jesus said, "Today salvation has come to this house because

this man is a son of Abraham, too. The Son of Man came to seek and to save that which was lost."

As soon as dinner was over, Zacchaeus found Peter because he seemed to be the spokesman for the group. Jesus himself was engaged in talking to salvation seekers.

"Who do I give my money to, so that it can be distributed to the poor?" he asked Peter.

"Judas carries the bag. I will try to find him," Peter said. He saw Simon in the crowd and asked him, "Simon, do you know where Judas is? Zacchaeus wants to give to the poor."

Simon replied, "I don't know. He was here earlier. He must have gone to buy food. He may not have known that we were eating at Zacchaeus' house."

"I'll just take it to the synagogue next Sabbath," Zacchaeus said. "Rabbi Omni is a good man. He really cares for the poor. He is so different from the rabbis at Jerusalem. He didn't even throw me out of the synagogue when I took this tax collecting job."

And so it was that had not Judas already gone to Elihu's house, there would have been plenty to replenish the empty bag.

CHAPTER 27

THE BEGINNING OF THE END

Judas knocked at Elihu's gate. A slave came and asked, "What do you want?"

"I want to see Elihu."

"Was he expecting you?"

Judas was getting impatient with the slave's impertinence. "No, but I have a very important message for him."

"Who are you, that I might tell him who is calling?"

"Judas of Iscariot!" He spoke louder than necessary. He was beginning to feel a little uneasy about his errand.

"My lord will see you." The slave was back and opened the gate. Judas followed the slave across an enormous courtyard and into a great hall that gave access to ten rooms. The house was even bigger and more elaborate than Judas had imagined it to be. The slave led the way into a large room where Elihu was seated on a high stool copying a scroll onto a new parchment. He stood and greeted Judas with a customary kiss.

"Anner, bring some water to wash our guest's feet and oil to anoint his face," Elihu commanded the slave and went back to penning his parchment while the slave carried out his orders.

"You have walked a long way, Judas?" Elihu's last sentence was in the form of a question.

"From Jericho," Judas replied. "I came to buy food for Jesus and his disciples."

"Are they here in Jerusalem?"

"No, they are still in Jericho."

"You came all the way to Jerusalem to buy food? Wasn't there any food in Jericho?" There was mockery in Elihu's voice. He knew that Judas had something else in mind.

"They will be here by sundown. They are coming with a party of pilgrims from Capernaum."

"Do you mean you came from Jericho alone? It is fortunate that robbers didn't kill you for what is in your bag." Unknowingly, Elihu had struck a nerve.

"The bag is empty." Judas blurted out the truth before thinking. Once he had started, he told Elihu the whole story, (what he hadn't dared tell the sympathizing Jesus) including his disillusionment with a kingdom of children, stupid fishermen and crooked tax collectors.

"I think I know a way you can fill the empty bag and stop this maniac from Nazareth at the same time," Elihu said. "Since Jesus raised Lazarus from the dead, the rulers are frantic. Sooner or later the Nazarene is going to cause a riot and the Roman government will deal harshly with the rulers, maybe the whole nation. They rule only on the condition that they maintain order. Rome has no patience with unrest and no mercy with insurrection. They won't even bother to find out who started it."

"What can I do?" Judas asked. "I can't stop him. If you had seen him do all the miracles that I have seen, you would know the impossibility of my doing anything."

"You know when he is alone and where. All we ask is that you lead us to him. We will do the rest." Elihu's use of the plural pronoun identified himself with the chief priests and rulers.

"How much would I get to do this?"

"I don't know. You will have to bargain with the priests after you have found out when and where he can be caught. In the meantime, go back and join the Group just as though nothing is different."

The interview was over. Elihu did not invite him to spend the night, nor did he recommend a place to stay. Judas could not go back down that Jericho road at night. It was dangerous enough in the daytime. Judas had no choice but to huddle in the shadows on a Jerusalem street. It was cold, almost as cold as it had been on the mountain.

The next day he retraced the road to Jericho. He met the Galilean party on the east side of Bethany.

"Where have you been, Judas? We've been looking all over for you," Simon said, but he didn't wait for an answer. "It's a good thing that you are here. We are all going to Bethany for a feast tonight. Martha is having a thanksgiving feast for Lazarus."

"I am happy to hear about that," Judas said with enthusiasm. "Martha is a good cook, and we always have plenty to eat at her house."

There were no more questions about his mysterious absence.

The Twelve left the Galilean party and stopped at Bethany. They arrived in the early afternoon and had time to rest before the feast.

"I wonder how long Bartimaeus had been by the highway at Jericho." Thomas and James were discussing the events of the morning.

"He had no doubt been there all night," James said. "He still had his cloak wrapped around him."

"He must have been cold last night," James said. "Those camp fires the Galilean party made felt pretty good." Judas was listening, but he made no comment. Simon apparently was the only one who had missed him from the Group.

"He had been sitting in that same spot for years," Bartholomew broke into the conversation. "I used to give him alms when I worked for Zaanan. He has to pay rent on it."

"Who would charge a blind man rent for a begging space?" asked James.

"I don't know, but that is what Bartimaeus told me. It is a good spot for begging. The crowds going up to Jerusalem to the Passover are in a very generous mood."

"I wonder who that other blind man was?" James asked.

"I don't know," Thomas said. "He may have come out from Jericho ahead of the crowd. Bartimaeus won't have to beg anymore."

"Begging is a poor way to make a living, but Bartimaeus had no other choice until Jesus came," James said.

They continued to discuss the events at Jericho, but nobody expected Judas to join in the conversation. He was usually moody and quiet. They were used to it. Sometimes he got into an argument with James and John, but even then he said what the rest were thinking. As a matter of fact, they liked Judas better than James and John. They deserved the nickname, "Sons of Thunder."

All afternoon people came from Jerusalem to Bethany. Of course, they weren't all going to eat, but they wanted to see Lazarus. That was all anybody could talk about at Jerusalem.

As the pilgrims arrived from Galilee, Perea and all the other provinces, those who had seen Jesus raise Lazarus spent hours telling the newcomers about it.

The whole city of Jerusalem was at a fever pitch.

Martha served a good dinner that evening, but it wasn't the feast that Simon had told Judas about. He had confused it with the Sabbath day feast that Simon, the leper, was giving tomorrow.

Simon had been healed at the beginning of Jesus' ministry in Galilee. He had been quite wealthy, but had been forced to give up his holdings when he developed the disease. He had gone to Galilee because lepers fared better there, where there were many grain fields to glean in. When Jesus had healed him, he returned to Bethany and resumed his former lifestyle. He had wanted to show Jesus his gratitude in a special way, but had lacked opportunity. When Lazarus had been raised from the dead, he began to plan a great feast to honor Lazarus, and to express his own thanksgiving.

There was a constant stream of curiosity seekers who had come out from Jerusalem to Bethany to see Lazarus. Because Jerusalem was more than a Sabbath day's journey from Bethany, they gathered at Simon's house as uninvited guests.

As the guests arrived, they took their places at the table with Simon occupying the host's place. Judas was assigned a place at Jesus' right. There was no more argument about chief places since Jesus had explained the servant nature of the kingdom.

Actually, they seemed to try to exceed one another in humility. Peter took a place at the foot of the table. Simon and Matthew were seated next to Judas and then James and John.

While they were eating, Mary brought in an alabaster box of spikenard, a very expensive perfume imported from India. Judas saw the box and knew what was in it. Although he had already discussed betraying Jesus with Elihu, he did not consider it binding until he had received the money for doing it. In the back of his mind, there was still hope that Jesus would establish a kingdom, but he knew that the stolen money would have to be replaced before he could have a part in it. After the Passover he would have to give an account of his management. Therefore, when Mary brought in the alabaster box, he saw an opportunity. If he could get to sell it and give to the poor, he would have enough to make up the shortage and much more. It was worth a year's wages.

What was she doing? She had poured that perfume on Jesus' head and feet!

"Why was this perfume wasted like this?" he almost shouted. "It could have been sold for three hundred denarii and the money given to the poor."

"Leave her alone," Jesus said. "There will always be poor people and you can give to them anytime you want. But I won't be with you much longer. She is anointing my body for burial. Wherever the good news is proclaimed, her act tonight will be told."

Judas had never been so humiliated in his life. As soon as the feast was over, he slipped away to Jerusalem to bargain with the priests. As he approached a priest in the temple, he was totally unprepared for the haughtiness with which he was received. He had forgotten how condescending they were.

"Who are you?" Annas asked coldly.

"I am Judas of Iscariot," Judas replied, wishing he hadn't come.

"We have no interest in speaking with a publican," Annas spat in disgust. So they did know who he was.

"Didn't Elihu tell you about the agreement we had made?" Judas replied irritably. He didn't like being put down.

Annas sensed that he was pushing Judas a little too far and backed off a little. "I believe Elihu did mention a disciple of the Nazarene who might be able to help us stop that maniac. Do you have a plan?"

"He goes to a solitary place to pray every night, but I won't know where until I know where we are staying. When we are at Jerusalem, he goes to the garden of Gethsemane."

"When you find out, come back here and we will send our Temple guards to arrest him." Annas turned and walked away.

"Elihu said that there would be money in it for me!" Judas shouted after him.

"You will get your money when you come back with more definite information."

Judas walked out of the temple very agitated. The humiliation at Simon the leper's house, the arrogance of Annas, and the disgust with what he was doing were straining his emotions. He hated Annas, he hated himself, and he was disillusioned with the kingdom idea.

He went back to Bethany and found the disciples at Martha's house. There was still a crowd of curiosity seekers talking to Lazarus. No one had missed him.

After most of the visitors had found places to stay with relatives or friends for the night, the Twelve built a small fire in the courtyard and curled up in their cloaks to sleep.

CHAPTER 28

THE KING IS COMING

Martha cooked over the open fire in the courtyard. After they had all eaten, they sat around a long time. More and more people came to the house to see Lazarus. When the courtyard was filled, Jesus left with his disciples and the crowd followed him. When they reached the outskirts of the village, Jesus stopped and called Simon and Judas.

"Go to Bethpage," he commanded. "As you enter the village, you will find a donkey mare tied with a colt beside her. Untie her and bring them to me. If anyone questions you, tell them that the Lord needs the colt and he will let you take them."

Simon and Judas went to Bethpage, which was only a short distance north of Bethany. Just as Jesus had said, they found the donkey mare with the colt beside her. When they untied her, a man said, "What are you doing?"

"The Lord needs the colt," Simon replied. The man said no more, and they went back toward Bethany leading the donkey with the colt following.

They met Jesus and the crowd just before they crested the Mount of Olives. Jesus put his cloak on the colt and spoke softly to him, then got astride him. The colt was nearly grown, but still Jesus' feet were barely off the ground. The colt started walking up the road toward Jerusalem as though he had been trained to carry a rider. The mother followed behind without braying or protesting.

A crowd was now coming from Jerusalem. They broke off branches from palm trees and spread them in the road ahead of the colt. They also spread their garments in the road so as to almost make a carpet for the colt to walk upon. The colt walked slowly along, as though he knew he was carrying a king.

As they topped the ridge and began descending the west slope of the Mount of Olives, they caught the first glimpse of the city of Jerusalem, a city of palaces, from the palace of the Maccabees to that of the high priest. The castle, where Herod lived, was supposedly built on the very site of the Palace of King David.

As the city came into view, the crowd took up a chant: "Hosanna to the Son of David!"

From the crowd at the head of the column: "Blessed is he that comes in the name of the Lord!"

Those following answered: "Blessed be the kingdom that comes, the kingdom of our father, David!"

Answer: "Blessed be he that comes in the Name of the Lord!"

Chorus: "Hosanna! Hosanna in the highest!"

Answer: "Peace in heaven and glory in the highest!"

At last the day of crowning had come. Judas began to have second thoughts about his bargain with Elihu and the priests. Well, no money had changed hands. He didn't have to do it. They could try to catch Jesus without his help. No one would have to know that he had considered betraying Jesus. The rest of the disciples had no inkling that he had talked to the priests, and the priests would not want them to find out because their plot depended on secrecy.

His wandering mind was focused by a priest elbowing his way toward Jesus, and his heart came up in his throat. It was Annas. It was all over; Annas was going to tell Jesus about his being at the temple last night. Although the crowd continued their chant, he could hear Annas say, "Make these people be quiet!"

Jesus replied, "If these people were quiet, the very stones would cry out."

Annas hadn't said what Judas feared, and he melted back into the crowd, relieved.

Just then the colt came to the crest of another rise in the road and the whole city came into view. At this point, the entire Kidron Valley can be seen. Its great depth as it joins the valley of Hinmon gives the illusion of a city rising out of a deep abyss.

At the first sight of the city, Jesus cried, "O, Jerusalem, Jerusalem, you that kill prophets and stone the messengers that are sent to you by God. How often I wanted to gather you together as a hen her chicks, but you would not. Your whole family will be abandoned. You will not see me anymore until you will say, 'Blessed is he that comes in the name of the Lord.'" As Jesus finished uttering these words, he sobbed great sobs that shook his entire body, sobs of grief at the death of a loved one.

The disciples were puzzled. The city from this view was beautiful, and he was surrounded by throngs of joyful people. When the sobs subsided, he rode quietly down the slope, through the Golden Gate, and up to the Temple. Some, but not nearly all, of the people followed him through the gate and up to the Temple.

The sun was now sinking in the West and Jesus took the Twelve and went back to Bethany for the night. He made no effort to claim the throne, or even go to the palace.

CHAPTER 29

COUNTDOWN TO MISERY

Elihu had been in the crowd that accompanied Jesus into Jerusalem. The priests had enlisted him to watch Jesus' movements. He no longer had any desire to become part of Jesus' kingdom, but he had been impressed with the demonstration of the people that day. Of course, almost all those who took part in the parade were from Galilee and Perea. They had come to be at the Passover feast and heard about the raising of Lazarus. They were uneducated farmers and fishermen. None of the wealthy influential people of Judea were swayed by his entry into Jerusalem.

Elihu had to admit that Jesus was an amazing person, but, as the rulers said, he couldn't be permitted to raise a rabble in Jerusalem. Too bad Jesus hadn't stayed out in the provinces where he could have worked his miracles and not caused any disturbances. It was too bad he had to die in the prime of life. He was so talented.

"Look, you have accomplished nothing. The whole world is following him!" Dodai, a ruler, was yelling at Elihu. He seemed to think that Elihu should do something about it.

"Didn't Judas ever come to the Temple?" Elihu asked.

"One of Jesus' disciples did come in and talk to Annas, but I don't know what he said," Dodai replied. Elihu said nothing more, but decided to talk to Annas at the first opportunity.

After Jesus and the Twelve had gone back to Bethany, Elihu went to make his report. Annas had been high priest, but Caiphas, his son-in-law, was now serving in that office. However, Annas still had considerable influence, and Caiphas usually checked with him before he did anything important.

"Elihu, what have you got to report today? It seems to me that we are getting nowhere in catching the Nazarene. In fact, the crowds around him are getting larger all the time." Annas' tone was accusing.

Elihu was not to be cowed. "Didn't Judas of Iscariot talk to you?"

"We can't do business with a publican!"

"I don't think we can do business with anyone else. The rest of the disciples are ready to die with and for Jesus." Elihu spoke as respectfully as he could.

"I'll discuss it with the others tomorrow," Annas said, toning his voice down.

Elihu was disgusted with the old priest. He had cultivated Judas' friendship, and now when Judas was about to agree to betray Jesus, Annas had offended Judas because he had been a publican. Perhaps it would be easier to work with Caiphas. Caiphas believed that Jesus would have to die for the people. To allow him to continue would bring destruction of the whole Jewish nation from Rome. Rome would not tolerate any kind of uprising.

Judas was hungry. They had camped on the Mount of Olives last night, but they had no food. Not as bad as the cold, dark mountains, but if he could just get enough money to buy or bribe his way into a tax booth, he would get back into the business. Matthew had mentioned a publican on the east side of Capernaum who was interested in becoming a disciple.

The sun was pleasantly warm on their backs. It had just risen and was chasing the night chill away, but not high enough to be hot. They caught sight of a lone fig tree ahead of them. It already had leaves, which was unusual for this early in the spring. Jesus and the Twelve quickened their steps. They were hungry and had reason to believe that the tree would have well-ripened figs on it, since a fig tree sets on fruit before the leaves put out. Running on ahead, Peter climbed the tree, but could find no figs on it. They were all disappointed, but Jesus was genuinely upset. "May no one ever eat fruit from you again!" he said.

They continued on their way to Jerusalem. Judas sensed that something dramatic was going to happen that day. Jesus had gone into the Temple and looked around, but said nothing. It had been late afternoon, but now he had the whole day before him. Perhaps today would be the day when Jesus would finally establish his kingdom. Tonight they might stay in the palace, instead of camping on the Mount of Olives. Judas didn't know why he kept daydreaming about a kingdom that he had virtually renounced when he had approached Annas. He hoped he never saw that old Pharisee again. The very idea, calling him a "publican." So what was wrong with being a publican? If Jesus didn't establish the Kingdom today, he would go back to the publican business.

When Jesus arrived at the Temple area, he fashioned a whip out of cords and started driving out the cattle. He didn't need to use the whip; at the sight of their creator, they trampled each other to get out into the streets. He went inside and overturned the money-changers' tables and released the doves from their cages.

"It is written, 'My house shall be called a house of prayer,' but you have made it a den of robbers!" Jesus said angrily.

The peddlers went scurrying out like rats. When the sick and crippled saw the peddlers leave, they crowded into the space left by the cattle and the money-changers.

Some came leading blind people to be healed. While this was happening, a number of children, who had come in with crippled or blind parents, began to run up and down in the Temple shouting, "Hosanna to the Son of David."

Annas arrived at that time. "Do you hear what the children are saying?" he asked Jesus.

"Yes," replied Jesus. "Have you never read, 'From the lips of children and infants you have ordained praise'?"

Annas went back to his colleagues murmuring about the Temple being desecrated by all the shouting and dancing of the children.

Judas had been encouraged by Jesus' driving out the money-changers and the dove merchants. It was a step in the right direction, but it was not enough. A kingdom can't be built on blind people, cripples and children. Of course, Jesus had healed those who were crippled and blind, but it would be a long time before the children would be big enough to carry a sword or spear. Jesus had made no effort to depose King Herod or Pontius Pilate. It was the same old story. A lost opportunity. Jesus didn't know what he was doing. Did he expect Herod and Pilate to invite him up to the palace to take over the kingdom?

As if he knew what Judas had been thinking, Elihu came up behind him and said, "What will you take to help us catch Jesus alone?"

Judas was startled by Elihu's question, even though they had discussed it before. The sum that came to his mind was the sum of the contents of the bag before the dice game. "Three hundred denarii."

"That's a lot of money. A year's wages!" Elihu exclaimed.

"It's an awful thing you are asking me to do," Judas replied.

"All right, Annas is calling a meeting tonight to decide what to do with Jesus. I'll see what I can do for you," Elihu said as he walked away.

Judas' knees got weak and his hands trembled as he realized he had bargained away a friend's life. He sat down on one of the overturned benches.

"Come on, Judas, we are going back to Bethany tonight," Simon said. He was cheerful. He had been a zealot, and now he was even more enthusiastic about the Nazarene party. "Jesus put those money-changers and dove sellers out in a hurry."

"I was hoping he would take over the palace, too," Judas said.

"Oh, I am sure he will do that at the right time."

"This is the right time. He will never have a greater following than he has now. It seems to me that this is the best time, while all the people are here for the Passover."

"Jesus knows when is the best time, and he will do it when that time comes," Simon said with finality.

The sun was sinking behind them in the western sky as they went back to Bethany. Neither of them said any more. They had been together on apostolic treks long enough that Simon had learned to expect and respect Judas' moodiness.

The morning dawned bright and clear. All the disciples were light-hearted and cheerful except Judas. He was being carried along by events that arose out of his own wrong decisions. There seemed to be no way out now. He felt himself more of a spectator than a participant in the events of the days that followed.

"Teacher! Look! The fig tree that you cursed is withered!" Peter exclaimed.

"Have faith in God," Jesus answered. "I'm telling you the truth. If anyone would say to this mountain, 'Go throw yourself into the ocean,' and doesn't doubt in his heart, it will happen. Whatever you ask in prayer, believe that you have received it and it will be yours. And when you pray, if you have anything against anyone, forgive him, so that your Father in heaven can forgive you your sins."

Just as Elihu had told Judas, there had been a meeting at the high priest's palace to decide what to do with Jesus. Annas and Caiphas, other priests, Pharisees and scribes, Elihu, money-changers, dove merchants, all had come together to plan a way to get rid of the troublemaker.

"If we can get him in trouble with the Roman government, they will take care of the problem and his blood won't be on our hands," advised Jonathan, the high priest during the reign of Herod the Great. "I will ask him if it is lawful to pay tax to Rome. If he says, 'Yes,' he will be in trouble with his own followers. Some of them have barely enough to eat after they have paid their taxes. If he says, 'No,' Roman soldiers will take him away."

"That is a good idea, Jonathan," said Caiphas, who was in charge of the meeting.

"I'm going to challenge his authority. He chased the money-changers out of the Temple this afternoon as if the Temple belonged to him. He gets his power from Beelzebub. If we can get him to admit it, his followers will desert him, because they think he gets his power from God," Annas said with vehemence.

"Very good," Caiphas said. "Are there any other ideas?"

Elihu was very careful in his deference. "I feel that I have no right to speak in so august company. But Judas of Iscariot would be willing to betray Jesus for a price."

"We will not deal with a publican," Annas fumed. "Certainly not for a price!"

Caiphas was more diplomatic. "We will do what is necessary to trap the Nazarene," he said.

No decision was made, and Elihu left without anything definite to offer Judas. The next morning when he went to the Temple, he found Annas and Jonathan already there. Caiphas was not present. Jonathan had enlisted some Herodians to help carry out his plan because he didn't want to be too closely identified with the nationalistic party.

They went to the Gentile area of the Temple where Jesus had driven out the cattle the day before. They blocked Jesus' way into the Temple, and Annas spoke out belligerently, "Who gave you the authority to drive out the cattle and overturn the money tables?"

Jesus replied calmly, "I will ask you one question. Answer me, and I will tell you by what authority I am doing these things. John's baptism, was it from God or from men? Tell me."

They went into a huddle, and Jesus stood quietly waiting for their answer.

Jonathan said, "I don't know how we are going to answer him. If we say, 'from heaven,' he will say, 'Then why didn't you believe him?' If we say, 'from men,' everybody in Jerusalem believes that John was a prophet."

So Annas answered Jesus, "We don't know."

"Then I won't tell you by what authority I am doing these things." Jesus moved past them into the Temple.

"What are we going to do now?" Elihu asked.

"Janner is going to ask him about paying taxes to Caesar," Jonathan said. "Jesus doesn't know him. He is a Herodian from Galilee. Jesus will not expect a trick question from a Galileean."

Jesus was teaching a parable when they approached him in the Temple. He was saying, "Some they beat, others they killed. Finally, he sent his son, saying, 'They will surely respect my son.' But the

tenants said to one another, 'This is the heir. Let's kill him, and
the inheritance will be ours.' That is what they did and threw his
body out of the vineyard. What do you suppose the owner did?
He came and killed those wicked tenants and rented his vineyard
to others. Haven't you read the Scripture: 'The stone that the
builders rejected has become the capstone;' the Lord has done
this, and it is marvelous in your eyes?"

Janner stepped out of the crowd and said, "Teacher, I would
like to ask a question."

Jesus turned to him politely and said, "Go ahead."

"We know that you are a man of integrity. You aren't swayed
by men's opinions because you pay no attention to their rank or
station, but you teach the way of God according to the truth. Is it
right to pay taxes to Caesar or not?"

"You are trying to trap me," Jesus said. "Bring me a denarius."
Janner handed him a coin.

"Whose picture is on this coin?"

"Caesar's."

"Give Caesar what belongs to him and to God what is his."

Annas' plan hadn't worked. Now, Jonathan's had failed. They
were stymied. But the Sadducees, who say there is no resurrection,
thought that they could succeed where the Pharisees had failed.
They had always bested the Pharisees in one hypothetical question
about the resurrection.

Confident that he would confuse Jesus, Zether stepped forward
and said, "Teacher, we know of a man who died without having
any children. His brother married his widow in the hope of bringing
a son into the world to bear the dead man's name. Unfortunately,
he died, too, without having any children. There were seven of
these brothers. All married the woman, but none had any children.
At last, the woman died, too. The question is: Whose wife will she
be in the resurrection?"

Jesus replied, "You have a mistaken idea of the resurrection,
because you don't understand the Scriptures nor the power of God.
When the dead rise, they will be like the angels. Marriage is an
earthly relationship that no longer exists in heaven. About the

dead rising, haven't you read about Moses meeting God in the burning bush? God said to him, 'I am the God of Abraham, the God of Isaac and the God of Jacob.' He is not the God of the dead, but of the living."

Elihu couldn't help admiring Jesus' reply to Zether. He had discussed the same question with the Sadducees before. He knew the Scriptures well, but that interpretation had never occurred to him. He stepped forward to ask Jesus a question.

"Of all the commandments, which is the most important?"

Of course, Jesus remembered Elihu as the scribe who was unwilling to be without a home, but without referring to that episode, he gave Elihu a simple answer. "The most important commandment is this: 'Hear, O Israel, the Lord our God is one God. You shall love the Lord your God with all your soul and with all your mind and with all your strength.' The second is this: 'Love your neighbor as yourself.' There are no greater commandments than these."

"That's right, Teacher. God is one God and there are no other Gods. To love him is more important than burnt offerings and sacrifices."

"You are not far from the Kingdom of God," Jesus said.

Elihu felt a strange tugging at his heart. This Jesus of Nazareth fitted his own conception of the Messiah. For a fleeting moment, he had a great yearning to renounce all the trappings of the priesthood, all the empty rituals and ceremonies and follow Jesus.

Annas took hold of his arm and said, "Come, Elihu, let's go talk some more with Caiphas about your plan." Elihu had forgotten in the heat of the debate what Annas was talking about.

As soon as they arrived at the high priest's palace, Caiphas opened the discussion. "You said that Judas of Iscariot would betray Jesus for a price. What is that price?"

"Three hundred denarii," Elihu replied.

"We can't pay him that much money. I don't see how we can pay him any money. It would be blood money," Caiphas protested.

Jonathan came up with a solution. "The law does not apply to slaves. We can buy Jesus as a slave, and it wouldn't be blood money."

"Nobody would pay three hundred denarii for a slave!" Annas exclaimed.

"Slaves are selling for thirty shekels. Let's give him that amount," Caiphas said. "Elihu, go get Judas and bring him here."

Elihu found Judas in the Temple with the other Twelve. There was still a crowd listening to Jesus teaching, and Judas left with Elihu without anyone noticing.

Judas noticed a marked difference in Annas' and Caiphas' and Jonathan's attitude. They seemed glad to see him.

"Here is the money," Annas said. "All you have to do is lead us to Jesus when the crowds are not around."

Judas nodded. He didn't bother to count the money. He knew without counting it that it was not nearly enough to cover his gambling loss, but he no longer cared. He felt like an actor in a dream. Like Esau of old he had sold his birthright for a mess of pottage.

He slipped back into the Temple without anyone being aware that he had been gone.

Jesus was speaking," Woe unto you teachers of the Law and you Pharisees! You are all hypocrites! You build tombs for the prophets and decorate the graves of the righteous. You say that if you had lived in the days of your forefathers, you would have had no part in killing the prophets. But, really, you are no different from them. You are planning to finish filling the measure of sin that they started!

"You snakes! You brood of vipers! How can you escape the condemnation to hell? Therefore, I'm sending you prophets and wise men and teachers. Some of them you will kill and crucify, and others you will flog in your synagogues and pursue from town to town. And so upon you will come all the righteous blood that has been shed on the earth, from the blood of righteous Abel to the blood of Zechariah, who you murdered between the Temple and the Altar. I tell you the truth, all this guilt will fall on this generation."

When Jesus had finished his appeal, he left the Temple through the Golden Gate. Crossing the black Kidron Valley, they could look back across the valley and see the evening sun shining on the temple walls and spires.

"Look, teacher, what massive walls," Matthew exclaimed.

"There will not be one stone left upon another," replied Jesus.

Peter, James, John and Andrew sat down, but Judas and the other disciples continued on down the road toward Bethany.

They didn't talk, just walked along silently with Judas, each buried in his own thoughts. So much had happened that day, so many things that Jesus had said that they couldn't comprehend. They seemed not to notice that four of their number were asking Jesus about even more incomprehensible things, future events that remain a mystery even to this day.

Judas had missed most of Jesus' teaching in the Temple. He had never been interested in his teaching, even less so now that he had crossed the line from being a half-hearted disciple to a secret enemy of Jesus. Of course, he didn't think of himself as an enemy. He was participating in the inevitable. Jesus was just dreaming, if in fact, he had any intentions of being a king. He seemed determined to infuriate the rulers. The way he had berated the Pharisees in the Temple would not help his cause at all. The high priest and elders had already decided to arrest Jesus. They would have found a way to do it without Judas' help. Someone else would have done it if he hadn't. Peter, Andrew, James and John were thoroughly convinced that Jesus was going to be king. They were back there right now, hanging onto his every word.

But, what about those others who were walking along with him? He hadn't asked them to come. Why hadn't they stayed back there with those four dreamers who thought Jesus was God? He knew that Thomas had his doubts. He wondered what Philip, Simon, Matthew or any of the others would have done if Elihu had approached one of them. But why did it have to be him! He was almost thinking aloud. A quiet sigh escaped his lips.

"Something wrong, Judas?" inquired Nathaniel.

"Oh, no, I guess I'm just tired."

"Me, too. I'll be glad to get to Bethany and some of Martha's cooking."

"We should wait until Jesus and the rest catch up," Philip said.

"At least we can get a drink and wash our feet," Nathaniel replied. Philip and Nathaniel kept up the conversation, and Judas lapsed back into his dismal mood.

The sun was setting as Jesus and the other four disciples arrived. Martha served lentils and bread in the courtyard.

After they had eaten, Jesus taught them in parables about the kingdom. Judas was no longer interested in the kingdom. It was all nonsense, anyway. Something about five foolish bridesmaids. Judas gathered that Jesus intended to go away after the Passover. Evidently, he was going alone. He talked about giving talents. Where would he get that kind of money? A talent was ten times what Judas had lost gambling. Oh, well, never mind, he might just take his thirty shekels and try to get back into the publican business.

The following day they didn't go to the Temple. They didn't do much of anything. The long-needed rest that Jesus had promised them at Capernaum had come at last. They just sat around under the trees on the Mount of Olives. There were still many people passing on the road between Jerusalem and Bethany, but they evidently didn't notice the Twelve.

At one point Jesus called them together and said, "You know that two days from now will be Passover. The Son of Man will be betrayed and crucified."

Judas' heart came up into his throat. Jesus knew that he was going to betray him! How did he find out? Someone must have seen him go into the high priest's palace. But they wouldn't know what was said unless someone in the palace had told Jesus, but none there would have wanted Jesus to find out. No one had said anything about crucifying Jesus. They had not even said anything about killing him, although Elihu had mentioned that possibility. Well, he had only agreed to lead them to Jesus. What they did after they arrested him was not his responsibility. He believed that Jesus would get a fair trial. He knew some of those on the Sanhedrin. Nicodemas and Joseph of Arimathea would never agree to the death penalty. Judas also knew that Caiphas and Annas hated Jesus, but they had no evidence of Jesus being guilty of anything deserving the death penalty.

Crucifixion! That was the Roman method of execution. The Sanhedrin did not have authority to crucify anyone. It was obvious that Jesus didn't know what he was talking about.

He became conscious of a conversation between Peter and Andrew.

"I can't understand why anyone would want to tear down that beautiful Temple," Andrew was saying.

"Jesus said that we would see it in our lifetime," Peter replied. "When we see Jerusalem surrounded by armies, we are to escape to the mountains."

"I wonder if that will happen before all nations will be brought before the Son of Man for judgment," Andrew mused.

"I don't know, but I sure wouldn't want to be on the goat side."

"We don't have to worry about that; we have been disciples from the beginning."

"Don't be too sure. Jesus said that many will say to me on that day, 'Lord, Lord, did we not prophecy in your name, and in your name drive out demons and perform many miracles?' Then I will tell them plainly, 'I never knew you. Get away from me, you evildoers.' You remember his saying that, don't you?"

"He was talking about false prophets then."

"He wasn't talking about false prophets when he said, 'I have chosen twelve of you and one of you is a devil.'"

Judas moved away. He didn't want to hear anymore. He knew who Jesus meant the day he had spoken those words, but he had dismissed it from his mind. He hadn't done anything wrong; but now, he just wished he had never seen that scribe, Elihu. That was it. Elihu was the one who had suggested that he betray Jesus, so he was the one to blame for it.

The Twelve did not go back to Bethany that evening, but ate what they had in their baskets. There seemed to always be a little something in their baskets since Jesus had fed the five thousand. It was not miraculous, but they had gotten into the habit of gathering fruit and grain as they traveled (it was permissible to glean after the harvest) and saving the leftovers from their meals. Sometimes the food spoiled, and they had to throw it away, but they learned to dry the fruit and to grind the meal as they used it.

When the meager meal was finished, Jesus led them to a secluded garden called Gethsemane, where they usually went to pray when they were in Jerusalem. It belonged to Adaliah, who was in the crowd of Lazarus' tomb when Jesus raised him from the dead. He had become a believer and was very delighted to have Jesus and the Twelve use it as a prayer garden.

"There is only one path into the garden, and I will see that you are not disturbed," Adaliah assured Jesus.

"We will not need it after tomorrow evening," Jesus said.

"Must you leave so soon? I was hoping that you might stay at Bethany for a long time," Adaliah said.

"It is expedient that I go away," Jesus replied.

They excused themselves and walked up the path into the garden. Although the moon was full, the canopy formed by the dense foliage of the olive trees caused it to be dark in the garden. Each found a place to pray. Judas did not pray, indeed could not pray. He could hear the others pray and recognized their voices. Jesus was a little farther in the garden than the rest, but his voice carried above the others, although the leaves of the trees muffled its normally clear and distinct tones. Judas heard Jesus mention his name, but could not understand the other words. However, from the intonation, it was an earnest, pleading intercession for him. He felt a compelling desire to slip over to Jesus and confess the whole sordid affair. But, no, he would not interrupt Jesus' praying; instead, he slipped out of the garden where he could no longer hear anyone praying. After about an hour, the rest filed out of the garden with Jesus in the lead. Judas joined their ranks and no one suspected that he had not been in the garden the entire time. They went back to their daytime camp on Olivet.

"That was a perfect place to pray," John said. "It was like having our own private temple."

Jesus said, "We will go back tomorrow evening."

Judas didn't sleep any that night. The turmoil and torture of conflicting emotions kept revolving in his mind. "All you have to do is lead us to him" had seemed simple, yet indefinite when Annas had said it. Heretofore, he had not had opportunity, but now, it lay before him. He could lead them into the garden tomorrow night. There would be no crowds around. So simple, yet so fearful. He was going to do it, and yet he didn't want to. But that agreement had been made. The money was already in the bag.

CHAPTER 30

POINT OF NO RETURN

The hooves of a donkey ringing on the stones awakened the Twelve to the new day.

"Shalom, my brothers. I have brought you something to begin the day with," Adaliah greeted them. He had brought thirteen freshly baked unleavened cakes, four large fish and a jar of goat's milk.

Jesus was still asleep, but awakened by Adaliah's voice, he smiled at him and said, "Adaliah, you are as welcome as the morning sun. Your generosity will not be forgotten."

Adaliah glowed in Jesus' appreciation. After the blessing, they all ate with gusto. Their meager meal of the evening before had not completely satisfied their hunger. Judas' sleeplessness had left him with a headache and a slight nausea. Nevertheless, he forced himself to eat to avoid any inquiry about his appetite. He felt better after he had eaten.

When they had finished, Jesus called Peter and John. "Go, make preparations for us to eat the Passover."

"Where do you want us to prepare for it?" they asked.

He replied, "As you enter the city, a man carrying a jar of water will meet you. Follow him to the house he enters, and say to the owner of the house, 'The Teacher asks: Where is the guest room? Where may I eat the Passover with my disciples?' He will show you a large upper room, all furnished. Make preparations there."

Peter and John found the man, a hired slave named Tobiah, carrying the jar of water as Jesus had said. Jonan, the owner of the house, showed them the upper room.

All arrangements had been made except for the lamb and bitter herbs. Tobiah, a believer, had a brother, Laban, who was a shepherd. He said, "I'll get a lamb from my brother and take it to the priests for approval. If you take it, they will pretend to find a blemish and reject it. My brother supplies lambs for the Temple. They know that any lamb that I bring will be from his flocks. He is not a believer, but he is honest and reliable and the priests trust him," Tobiah said. "You could buy one that is already approved, but they would charge you an outrageous price for it."

Jonan was also a disciple, as was his son, Mark. He invited them into his own living quarters (the upper room was reached by an outside stairway and was not connected otherwise to the rest of the house) until Tobiah returned with the lamb.

"Tell me all you can about Jesus," Jonan said. "I was at Bethany when he raised Lazarus from the grave. Lazarus was my friend. I was with him when he died."

"We don't know where to begin," Peter said. "It would take a week to tell it all. I was a fisherman when he called me. He is the most amazing man I have ever met. I believe he is the Messiah, the son of the living God."

"I believe that he was in the beginning with God and he was God," John said. "All things were made by him."

"Then you believe that he is God?" Jonan said.

"No mere human being could have done all the things that I have seen him do," Peter said.

"Some of the old prophets worked miracles," Jonan said.

"None of the old prophets claimed a prior existence, but Jesus said, 'Before Abraham, I am,'" John explained.

"Then the rulers imagine a vain thing. They intend to kill Jesus, but God can't be killed," Jonan reasoned.

"Jesus said that they would kill him and that he would rise again in three days, but I don't know what he meant," Peter said. "When I tried to rebuke him, he called me Satan."

"I, too, believe that he is the Son of the living God," Jonan confessed.

Tobiah returned with the lamb, and Peter and John took it to the Temple to get it killed so that they could get it roasted in time for the Passover supper that evening. There were two long lines of worshippers with lambs to be killed. The lambs did not bleat nor struggle as they were passed from the worshippers to the priests, who killed them and passed the blood on to other priests to pour out on the altar. After removing the head and kidneys to be burned on the altar, the priest gave the lamb back to Peter and John, who returned to Jonan's house. Tobiah took the lamb and roasted it on an outdoor spit that Jonan had made for that purpose.

Jesus and the rest of the Twelve came into the courtyard just as Tobiah had finished roasting the lamb. The sun had already slipped below the horizon as they ascended the steps to Jonan's upper room. There were thirteen cushions arranged around a low horseshoe-shaped table, four on each side and five at one end. The other end of the table was left open in order that a servant could bring food to the table without stepping on any of the guests, who lay on their left sides on the cushions.

Evidently, Jesus' teaching about how greatness in the Kingdom came by being the least had been taken literally by the Twelve because Peter went around to the least esteemed place. John might have followed, but Jesus lay a restraining hand on his shoulder. Jesus lay on a cushion from the right and motioned for John to take a place at his right. All the rest took places as they came to them, leaving a space at Jesus' left open. Judas took the empty place, not that it made any difference anymore. James had expected his brother to take a place on the far side of the table with him and Peter. He controlled his jealousy when John had taken a place at Jesus' right hand, but when Judas lay at Jesus' left hand, he could contain it no longer. "Who do you think you are?" he bristled at Judas. "What have you ever done to deserve the chief seat?"

"You always get the chief seat," Judas said, and then taunted, "Your mother isn't here tonight to beg for you."

James said no more. He remembered too well the humiliation he felt when Jesus had said, "To sit on my right or left is not mine to give." Jesus did not address their quarreling. He just looked pained. He waited until all had reclined at the table and then he said, "One of you will betray me." They all looked at him with incredulity and said, "Is it I, Lord?"

Jesus answered, "It is the one to when I will give the sop. The Son of Man goes as it is written of him. But indescribable anguish is ahead for him who betrays the Son of Man. It would have been better for him if he had never been born."

A sickening feeling rushed over Judas. He had never realized until now how serious was the act that he was about to commit. Although he had been pretty certain all along that Jesus knew about the stolen money, he hadn't thought of his bargain with the Jewish leaders as being a betrayal. He was shaken to the very marrow of his being. But Jesus hadn't actually pointed him out. They had all asked, "Is it I?" Evidently, they all felt as guilty as he did. In the nightmare that he was now dreaming, he saw Peter motion across the table to John and John whisper to Jesus.

Judas had to find out for sure that Jesus really knew who was going to betray him. "Is it I, Lord?" he whispered to Jesus.

"You have said it," Jesus whispered back, and then said aloud to all of them, "It is the one to whom I will give a sop."

As Jesus dipped the bread into the bowl of bitter herbs, lamb pieces and salt, Judas saw all the symbolism it meant to whom it was given: I love you and I am willing to die for you. The symbolism was lost to the understanding of the rest, because the host customarily served the one to the right and left before he ate. Judas could hardly swallow it.

"What you are going to do, do it quickly," Jesus said. Judas escaped on wooden legs. He seemed to be carried on by a force beyond himself.

CHAPTER 31

HORRIBLE DEATH

Judas was very agitated. He had gone straight to Annas' house after he had left the upper room. He had knocked on the gate a long time before a servant came to answer it.

"My master is at prayers now, and he can't be disturbed," he said. "Come back later."

"Tell him that it is Judas of Iscariot, and that I have very important business."

"I cannot disturb him now. I will tell him that you have been here," the servant replied and left Judas standing outside the gate.

After what seemed a long time to Judas, although probably only about twenty minutes, the servant reappeared and ushered Judas into Annas' room.

"I was wondering if you were going to keep your bargain," Annas began haughtily. "We should never have given you the money until you had led us to him." At any other time Judas would have burned, but he didn't care anymore; he just wanted to get the dirty business over.

"Jesus is going to the garden of Gethsemane to pray. Although the moon is shining brightly, it will be dark in the olive grove. I will go to him and kiss him, so you will know which one is him."

"I'm not going out there with just a few servants," Annas replied. "I will send for the palace guard and as many others as can be found."

"But there are only twelve of them, including Jesus. I don't think he will resist arrest." Judas found himself hoping that Jesus would escape.

"I'm not taking any chances. He has escaped us before," Annas insisted. "Don't try to tell me how to run my business."

Judas was ushered into another room to wait for Annas to marshal his troops. After about an hour, he could hear the babble of many voices and smell the acrid odor of burning tar. The same servant came and motioned for Judas to follow him. They went out to the gate, where about a hundred men were carrying clubs and staves. A few temple guards, who were allowed to carry swords by the Romans, were interspersed among the motley group. The servant took Judas to a tall man holding a torch in his hand and introduced him. "This is Malchus, who will go with you into the Garden of Gethsemane."

Judas nodded and Malchus gestured for Judas to lead them out. The boisterous crowd hushed as they left the city walls and descended into the Kidron Valley. Crossing the little brook, they ascended the path into the Garden.

Jesus and the eleven were standing just inside the Garden as though they were waiting for them. Judas, in a show of hollow affection, approached Jesus and said, "Teacher." Then he kissed him on the cheek.

"Judas, are you betraying the Son of Man with a kiss?" Jesus said. Sudden realization hit Judas and he turned and slipped back into the crowd.

"Who are you looking for?" Jesus asked Malchus.

"Jesus of Nazareth," Malchus replied.

"I am he," Jesus said. Malchus had never seen Jesus before. He was only doing what Annas had told him to do. He had supposed that Jesus was just another trouble-maker that he had to deal with to keep the Romans content. Now Jesus stood before him . . . calm, majestic and innocent in appearance. He understood now why the other temple guards had been unable to arrest Jesus. He shrank back from laying hands on him.

"Who is it you want?" Jesus asked again.

"Jesus of Nazareth."

"I told you I am he," Jesus replied. "If you are looking for me, let these men go."

Malchus started forward to take Jesus, but Simon Peter stepped out from behind Jesus and took a swing at Malchus with his sword. This was the first time that Peter had ever had a sword in his hand and he succeeded only in cutting off Malchus' ear.

"Put your sword away!" Jesus commanded Peter. "They that live by the sword, shall die by the sword." He then took the ear and reattached it to Malchus' head.

The Pharisees in the mob, seeing that Jesus did not intend to resist arrest, began to push forward.

"Am I a dangerous criminal," Jesus said, "that you have come out with swords and clubs to capture me?" Every day I was with you, teaching in the temple courts, and you did not arrest me. But this is your hour, when darkness reigns."

Then the temple soldiers tied Jesus. The rest of the disciples, including Peter, ran through the garden. The soldiers started to seize John Mark, who had followed the eleven from the upper room, but he left his tunic in their hands and ran away naked. They took Jesus back through the North gate into Jerusalem and to Annas' home. Annas himself answered the gate.

"Here is the prisoner," Malchus said.

"Take him to the palace. Caiphas will deal with him," Annas said.

Judas was numb. He had not expected Jesus to be arrested, although he had led the mob to him. Elisha had blinded an army; surely Jesus had more power than Elisha. He was filled with remorse as he trailed the soldiers to the palace. Since he was with the soldiers who had arrested Jesus, he was not challenged at the palace entrance and was allowed to go in with them.

The soldiers gathered around a fire that they had kindled in the courtyard. Judas stood back of the soldiers. Consequently, he received no benefit from the fire against the cold night air.

It reminded him of shivering all night on Mount Hermon, the night that he had first thought about leaving the chosen Twelve. Now it was final. He was on the other side, among Jesus' enemies. He wished that he was again with the disciples on Mount Hermon. Oh, if he hadn't gotten into that crap game! It was too late, now. Jesus was in there being questioned by Caiphas.

There was a knock at the gate. When the servant girl opened the gate, twenty-three priests and scribes of the Sanhedrin filed through into the palace. Judas recognized Elihu among them. So Elihu had been promoted to the prestigious Sanhedrin (maybe a reward for his part in the plot to capture Jesus). Judas was filled with loathing for the man. He felt used. And then the familiar sinking, sickening feeling of utter hopelessness gripped his heart. They were going to try Jesus, but there was no doubt about the verdict.

He saw John come out of the palace. He didn't know John was in there. He'd run away with the rest of them when Jesus was arrested. John went to the gate with the servant girl. She opened the gate and in came Peter. Peter came over to the fire, but he didn't see Judas. Malchus was standing with his back to the gate and didn't see Peter come to the fire. The servant girl followed Peter to the group standing around the fire and confronted him. "Aren't you one of the Nazarene's disciples?"

"No, I don't know the man," Peter said loudly.

"Didn't I see you in the garden with him?" Malchus recognized Peter when he spoke.

"I tell you, I don't know who the man is!" Peter left the fire and went back toward the gate.

A rooster crowed somewhere in back of the servant quarters.

"He was the one who tried to cut my head off in the Garden. I would have run him through with my sword if Jesus hadn't stopped him. He wasn't a very good swordsman; he only cut my ear off," Malchus chuckled.

"But you still have two ears; did you have three before?" another soldier teased.

"Jesus put it back on," Malchus said.

"Do you expect us to believe that?" the other laughed.

Malchus didn't answer, and there was a lull in the conversation around the fire, each man pondering in his own mind what had been said—if what Malchus had said was true. There was no reason to believe otherwise. The teasing was good-natured and in no way reflected the opinions of the other soldiers. Jesus did have miraculous power. Nevertheless, it had been dark in the garden, and the flickering torches had cast shadows that distorted figures and actions, making it difficult to be certain of anything.

Judas sank again into his hopeless despair. It all seemed to be some kind of nightmare. The figures around the fire, the girl at the gate, Simon Peter . . . all seemed far off actors on a stage.

"I said I didn't know the man! By the God in Heaven I swear I never saw him before!" The girl was again accusing Peter of being a disciple because he had a Galilean accent. The rooster crowed again. He seemed to know that daybreak was near, although it was still dark. The full moon was too near the western horizon to give any light.

The Sanhedrin came out of the palace. When the girl opened the gate to let them out, Peter rushed in front of them. Annas and Caiphas stayed behind. A thought suddenly occurred to Judas: If he could get Annas and Caiphas to change their minds, they might free Jesus. He followed them out the gate and into the temple. When Annas saw Judas following them, he turned and said, "What do you want? You have your money and you won't get any more."

"I have betrayed innocent blood. Here is your money back," Judas begged.

"That is nothing to us," Annas replied coldly.

Judas looked into Annas' eyes. They were cold and unfeeling. He could expect no pity from him, nor could Jesus. He could not change their minds, nor his fate. He felt the coins in the bag that he had carried three years for the little Group. He wouldn't be needing them in the place where he was going. He deliberately untied the mouth of the bag, and then grasping the bottom end, he swung it in a semi-circle. The coins struck the Temple floor and rolled in every direction. Dropping the empty bag, he turned and ran out of the Temple and through the western gate. He stopped to catch his breath. What to do now? It was over. Life was meaningless. The helpless, hopeless, sickening, sinking feeling of utter worthlessness again gripped his being. He hated himself. He hated Elihu. He hated Janus. He hated Annas, but he didn't hate Jesus. Whatever had possessed him to betray Jesus? It didn't occur to him that the devil had possessed him. He wanted to end his life, but how? And then he remembered a steep cliff overlooking the valley of Hinnom. He had seen it years ago. He had looked down from the wall of Jerusalem, which had been built on the edge of the cliff, and had seen the jagged rocks below. The rubbish had been carried through the dung gate, where there was a gradual descent into the valley. But here it was straight down to the rocks below. He would jump off the wall and end it all on those stones.

The eastern sky was growing pale, but going west he couldn't see too well. There it was, the rim with darkness beyond. He found a ladder that someone had left leaning against the inside of the wall, and climbed to the spot that he had remembered. He hurled himself into the dark abyss. A temporary weightless sensation surged in the pit of his stomach as gravity and momentum equalized, and then free fall. Something hit him in the stomach like a huge ram.

In the darkness, he had missed the spot overlooking the rocks; instead, he had thrown himself over a cliff that was not as steep. A few scraggly cedar trees had managed to grow in the thin soil at the bottom of the wall. The top of one had been struck by lightning the year before. The lightning had broken out the top, leaving a sharp stub pointing straight up. Upon this stub Judas had impaled himself. The initial shock had knocked him unconscious.

When he regained consciousness, he was hanging head down, and as he opened his eyes the early dawn revealed his own intestines hanging six inches from his face. He closed his eyes and vomited. The vomit ran out his mouth and nose and down into his eyes and hair. The hydrochloric acid began to sting his eyes.

With the rising of the sun came the flies . . . in swarms. They covered his exposed intestines and his face. He tried feebly to brush them away, but every movement only intensified the already excruciating pain.

The sun gained strength as it rose in the eastern sky and the heat added to Judas' misery.

He felt, rather than saw, the shadow that passed over his head, and the tree swayed slightly, but there was no wind. He opened his eyes to see what had caused the tree to sway. There, just below him, on a green branch untouched by lightning, was perched a huge vulture. The bird would cock his head one way and then another. An intense pain exploded in Judas' head. He cried out and the bird glided away, leaving Judas with one eyeball dangling down the side of his face.

As the sun rose higher and hotter he slipped into a delirium. He was at Gadera again. Jesus was exorcising the demons from the crazy man. Only, instead of going into the hogs, they were coming to get him. He regained consciousness once more to the seething, searing sea of pain. And then sunlight faded into blackness, and Judas was gone to his own place.

BVG